CONTENTS

THE PAINTINGS

CHAPTER ONE

It started off as any other normal, mundane Saturday as Billy Heath made his way to the Tally Community Centre for the start of his weekly art class. He'd started attending several weeks ago, after realising that in the nearly nine months that he'd lived in the city, the only friends he had, if they could really be called friends, was the pompous ass-hole in charge of finances and one of his fighter's girlfriends. Billy was young at only twenty-six, but he was a damn good boxing coach, and as such he knew that you don't become friends with the fighters, friendly yes, friends no, it makes it harder to yell things at them and work on an honest level.

He, like most twenty-six year old men, could only spend so much time locked away in a sweaty, dull gym before going nuts. It had been several years since his last real girlfriend, and the handful of one-night-stands in that time hadn't really done anything to erase the loneliness he dealt with on a daily basis.

The art class made perfect sense. It would be full of elderly people, which was a plus. Billy spent so much time away from the outside world he never felt he fit in with people his own age. Most of the CD's he owned were of bands who died in the late seventies. Most of the films he liked were in black and white (which most young people took to like Superman to Kryptonite), and of course no books were really any good for the first decade after they were released. He never felt more alone than when surrounded by people of his own age.

Billy figured that doing something creative and gentle around people who considered standing up out of a comfortable chair exercise would be a good departure from the daily grind of the boxing gym.

The small open room had the lingering smell of paint that had long since been absorbed into the walls. The rain outside pelting down onto the windows and the grey clouds overhead gave the place the appearance of dusk, even though it was only ten past one in the afternoon. Luckily, the room, and the whole building for that matter, was acclimatised for the abundance of old people, and so was comfortably warm, and any wetness on coats soon evaporated and dried out.

A bowl of fruit was perched upon a table, causing an inadvertent groan to escape from Billy's throat. Not that he was here for anything other than trying something new, but maybe a female model wouldn't go amiss? She doesn't even have to be naked, just not wearing too much. Hell, let her be wearing the fruit, just no more boring items like bowls or vases or, saints preserve us, random shapes in blues, reds, and yellows!

He settled in behind his easel, nodding a polite hello to Graham at his right. Graham was as nice a man as you'd ever like to meet. Short, slight pouch hidden under his shirt and wool vest, with a ring of white hair circling his head from temple-to-temple, and a moustache to match. Nice guy, oh, except that he was a massive bigot.

To Billy's left was a plump lady who had told Billy her name but he'd long forgotten it. She was fairly old, maybe the wrong side of sixty-five, who always wore too much of the type of perfume that made the wallpaper peel, and she applied her thick make-up with a trowel. As she smiled her grin at him, the lips pulling back to reveal slightly-yellowed false teeth, the thought of ever tasting that bright red lipstick made Billy queasy.

He dabbed the bristles of the brush into a splodge of blue paint and began to lifelessly stroke it across the blank canvas before him. How could this be losing its appeal so quickly? Billy asked himself. Maybe Billy did need the constant physicality to be truly taken with an activity? One of his guilty pleasures was being able to bench press just as much as some of the heavyweights. Knowing that he could lie his 170 pound frame down on its back and push so much iron above his chest that the fighters who weighed in excess of 240 were jealous was something that made him smile. He was proud of that.

The rain grew heavier and harder and was now pounding

down, bouncing off the roof of the community centre like a series of tiny drum strikes in a tin drum. The wind was causing the rain to smack against the window, periodically lashing against the glass like a slave master's whip.

It's pouring with rain, the old woman over there is eyeing me up like a basket of muffins and the old man on the other side of me is only a few seconds away from blaming the foul weather on immigrants or gays or the Jews. How did this happen to me? Billy often wondered what Graham thought of Sammy Davis Jr.

That was when she came in.

Maybe 5'4, long curly blond hair, her face partially obscured by her much too big red raincoat hood. Over her right shoulder hung her cream coloured handbag. Billy stared. The others in the class continued to paint their interpretations of the bowl full of fruit, but all Billy Heath could do was stare at the blonde in the red hood. A blob of blue paint fell from the bristles and landed on the floor besides Billy's feet.

'Hi,' the blond said pulling the hood from her head, revealing the most perfectly sculpted features on any face ever in the history of existence. She continued, 'Whew, coming down a storm out there.' Her accent was sexy to the point it could melt granite. Billy felt something in his stomach, or maybe just below it, where the old tribesmen believed a person's soul lived. He felt it whirling and glowing like a bright red-orange ball of desire in the pit of his gut.

She stood at the front of the room and took off her big red rain coat and hung it on the back of a chair, letting it drip-dry, forming a small pool on the laminated floor. She was wearing a long sleeve purple t-shirt, and blue jeans that hugged her hips and thighs invitingly.

'My name's Laurel,' she began. 'I'll be taking the art class from now on. Now don't worry, I may be young but I am fully qualified.'

'I'll bet you are,' Graham muttered under his breath.

Maybe fifteen minutes passed, with everyone in the room sinking deeper and deeper into their painting of the bowl of fruit. Billy hadn't done a single thing since the brush strokes quarter of an hour earlier. A lack of inspiration had taken control of Billy's brain and was refusing to let his arm move the brush over the canvas sheet.

'Well it's not as obvious as the others, but I like it.'

It was Laurel stood at Billy's side and looking at the thick blue rivers of paint that stretched out across his otherwise blank off-white canvas. Laurel pointed at the more crooked of the lines and, with a smile, commented, 'I take it this one's the banana?'

Billy blushed, cheeks turning a rosy red, and didn't know where to look for the moment. He used the wooden end of the brush to point at the fruit bowl and lamented that he was bored senseless and wanted, needed, something more intriguing to paint. Art is supposed to capture life, all this was doing was making him pray for mercy or beg for war.

'Okay,' Laurel said., clearly taken in by Billy's passion for the art. 'What would you like to paint?'

'No idea,' he lied, trying desperately not to look Laurel up and down like a starving man who's just seen a buffet. His eyes betrayed him and couldn't resist darting up and down her body, visually groping her curves and squeezing her breasts, cupping their curvature and circling the pebbles of her nipples.

'You know what I usually paint?'

'Walls?' Billy joked with a sly grin.

'Oh, very droll,' she smiled, a slight twinkle in her eyes. 'I paint the things I want to see.'

'Really?'

'Think about it.'

And with that, she smiled at him and, feeling a pleasurable

tingle tickling at her inner-thigh and groin, moved on around the class, checking everyone's work and progress. She had a point, and Billy thought it was a good idea and sound advice. Paint the things you want to see. So Billy thought about what he'd like to see. Painting Sammy Davis Jr tap-dancing on Graham the Bigot's head was ever-so-slightly out of his league. Painting Laurel, completely naked save for lipstick and high heels and smothered in clear honey might possibly give the game away and make future classes uncomfortable, and so that was also a non-starter.

Fuck it, he thought. I'll paint a sunny day.

Then the damndest thing happened. As he painted, the brush gliding easily from the paint to the canvas, the shapes beginning to take form, grew and began to come to life, the rain outside stopped. Only a few people noticed as most were engrossed in their own work. As Billy put the final touches to the somewhat crude rays of sunlight in his picture, he felt the ball of desire in his stomach grow in intensity and felt a similar ball growing just behind his forehead. He brought a hand up to his face to wipe away a swath of sweat that had started to pour from his pours, and accidentally slapped a smear of golden-yellow paint his cheek.

The room had grown so much hotter now in the last half an hour or so (ever since she'd spoken to Billy, in fact) that Laurel had unsightly dark patches under her arms, small enough not to make her un-sexy (if anything actually could), but it still looked as thought the purple shirt she wore was bleeding. She moved over to the window and opened it up without saying a word. There was no breeze.

Billy put his paints and brush down and removed his blue sweatshirt. He had a dark V shape of sweat on the back of his green t-shirt, and himself had the appearance of bleeding armpits.

Laurel caught sight of Billy, his tight t-shirt tucked into the waistline of his blue jeans, and she could tell he took good care of himself. She admired his broad shoulders and thick chest, his biceps were full and pumped, they had that vein that ran the length of the upper-arm and it was driving her crazy. She thought that Billy must spend considerable time working out. Laurel thought that she wouldn't mind having Billy work her out anytime he liked, and immediately blushed. Outside birds swooped down and pecked away at worms that were still on the ground after the rain.

Composing herself just enough to talk, Laurel declared to the class, 'That's your hour, I'm afraid.' Her voice echoed and bounced off the walls of the sparsely furnished room. The low murmur and clatter of people downing their palates and putting their coats on filled the room. The hushed-tone chatter of How did yours come out? Really? Mines too bad to look at-now tell me it's brilliant type conversations sounded dull in Billy's ears as though he were listening under water. He was mesmerised, staring at his painting through tunnel vision.

It was perfect. It was a masterpiece. It was the best work of art ever created within the walls of the Tally Community Centre. It was so life-like. My God, Bill, he told himself, you might just finally have found something you're very good at. But why's it just suddenly come out now?

Laurel had a polite, friendly smile on her face as she walked over to him. Her hair bobbed slightly, and he couldn't help noticing her breasts bobbed, too. Her. Billy knew the one thing different today was her. A muse, Bill. You've got yourself a muse.

'And how's yours?' she asked, breaking his concentration and well-aware of the innuendo within her words.

'What?' he asked startled.

'Your picture. How'd it turn out?'

'Oh, sorry.' Billy moved aside slightly, not that he needed to, and let Laurel get a good look at what he'd painted. In his mind Billy had thoughts of getting a good look as well, but not of anything that was on canvas. As he thought this an image played on the big screen in his head. He and Laurel were in a tent, miles away from civilisation. The were lying naked on a sleeping bag that was open and spread out. Their naked flesh pushed against each other, as their fingers traced small patterns over one another's bodies. His lips peppered her neck with shallow kisses, and moved down

her body, between her breasts and then lapping at her nipples (he envisioned her nipples as being very pink, and very erect) with his tongue.

Billy kept kissing her taut body and moved down towards her belly-button, all the while his fingers stroked teasingly at her ribs, her quick breaths and low groans were music to Billy's ears, he continued his nuzzling of her body and moved further south-

'Wow,' she said, bringing Billy back to the solid reality of the art class. 'That's really...why are you here?'

'Sorry?' Billy asked, trying to maintain eye contact with Laurel. If she kept eye contact then she wouldn't be able to look down and see just how happy Billy, or Little Billy, had been about the camping fantasy.

'Well, if you're painting like this you really shouldn't be in this class. You should be teaching it, not me.'

No, I...' Billy blushed again, he wasn't a man used to receiving compliments.

'Do you usually do so well?'

'No, no not usually. It's usually all crap.'

'A self-critic, too, eh?' she said placing squeezing Billy's triceps momentarily. 'So how come this was so good?'

'I...it was you,' Billy admitted, bowing his head. There was something very boyish, and appealing, about it for Laurel. It reminded her of when Popeye bashfully thrusts a bunch of roses at Olive Oil. Had they been alone in the room, Laurel would have pounced on Billy right there and worked the boy out of him, leaving him all man.

'Me?'

'Well, what you said, you know? Paint what you want to see.'

'Check me and my muse-self out,' she smiled and her face lit up. The smile seemed to stretch from ear-to-ear, her eyes were as wide as dinner plates. Billy wanted to take her in his arms and...well, although he wanted to spend a lot of time with her, he had a very strong urge right there and then to throw her down on the floor and fuck her brains out. He wanted to taste her, he wanted to fill her and fulfil her. He wanted to make her scream with orgasmic ecstasy as no man had made her do before. After a brief burst of nervous laughter from both, she asked, 'So what's your name? You haven't told me yet.'

'Sorry. I'm Billy. Billy Heath.'

As they shook hands Billy thought hers were the softest things he'd ever felt. The sensation of tingling, a thousand tiny, hot, pin-pricks under his skin ran from his hand up his arm. And somehow found its way to his groin. He felt the tingle flow down his penis, he felt the strange sensation of his balls tightening. He truly believed that Laurel had an amazing, magical power over him. Maybe she would inspire him to great works of art?

For Laurel, the same sensation ran through her body, making her nipples hard enough to be visible through he shirt, in spite of her thick, sensible bra. She felt herself growing moist and a burning ran up her thighs. If she was sure she would get away with it she would have taken Billy's hand and led his fingers over her body, down and into her.

'I should get going,' Billy said at last.

'Of course.'

They said their goodbyes and Billy left the class, headed for the fresh outdoor sun. Laurel sat down in the chair that she had hung her jacket on, and thought about the implications of starting an illicit affair with a student. She thought about whether or not those rules applied to a class full of people well-over eight-een. Mostly, however, she thought about the outline and size of the bulge she could see through Billy's jeans.

CHAPTER TWO

On the way home Billy could think of nothing else but the art, the great works of art he might have stored up inside that head of his. He decided to practice during the next week, nothing too complicated, but it had to be on par with Sunny Landscape that he'd created earlier. It would be impossible to get worse than a bowl of dying, dried up fruit, and Billy took consolation in that.

He stopped at an arts supply store and bought a palate, an easel, several pads of paper and brushes, and a handful of pots of primary colours. His plan was simple, if slightly immature in its naivety. He would, over the course of the next six days, practice painting one thing and one thing alone. Then, come next Satur-day he would paint it in class and impress the dress right off of Laurel.

Laurel. Thinking about her was making him tingle all over, and even when he'd been thinking about art is was with the desire to make Laurel want him. Oh, this was unbearable for Billy now, the pressure was building in his groin, his erection was almost painful.

'Excuse me,' Billy said to the man behind the counter of the arts and crafts shop. 'Do you have a bathroom I could use quickly? I don't think I'll make it home in time with all this stuff I've just bought.'

Cleverly done, Bill, he thought. He hoped that mentioning his large purchase would force the proprietor to allow him use of the facilities.

'Back there,' the proprietor said, pointing to a red-brown door twenty feet or so to Billy's right. 'Light's on a string just in-side the door.'

'Thanks,' Billy said and then went to the bathroom.

The toilet room was small, maybe only six feet by six feet, the lack of a basin made Billy cringe. The proprietor, the man who was exchanging cash with people all day long, had no place to wash his hands. Billy dropped his trousers to his ankles, and momentarily took in the sight with a great deal of pride. His manhood was being kept under control only by the stretching bright blue of his tight boxers, and it looked very good. Jesus Christ, Billy thought to himself. I've never seen it so big! With a broad smile plastered onto his face, Billy undid the button fly, whipped his impressively engorged pillar of passion out, and thinking of doing bad things with a good woman named Laurel, began to masturbate furiously. Every palm stroke in reality was a thrust in the fantasy. He could hear with amazing clarity the groans and moans Laurel should be, God-willing at some point would be, making in his ears. His forearm bulged with activity and never slowed for a moment as Billy brought himself to a knee-trembling, leg-weakening climax.

He came with such a force that his essence hit the toilet lid propped against the cistern and bounced off. He'd spent some considerable time alone before now, but he'd never had a session that ended with a ricochet before. It was a good feeling of relief that washed over him then, he saw bursts of bright light explode before his eyes in mid-air and let out an exhale of breath he hadn't even realised he was holding in. He put the seat and lid down and flushed the toilet, wishing there was a sink in the room to wash his hands, and wash away the sheen of sweat that had appeared on his forehead.

As Billy fumbled with all that he had just purchased, trying to figure the best way of holding onto everything and carry it without dropping everything and splattering the pavement tie-dye, he was hit with the reality of his predicament. What he was doing was all fine and well if he were a fourteen-year-old who'd seen his first glimpse of swollen bosom cleavage, but he was a grown man, for Christ's sake! What are you playing at? he asked himself. Then Laurel's face flashed across his mind's eye, and he knew he would be spending the next week painting.

It is almost, he thought momentarily, as though I have no choice in the matter.

***

Sunday morning, Billy went for his jog along the beach. The sand caught in his trainers and worked its way down his socks, chaffing between his toes, the way it did every week. Only this time Billy couldn't concentrate on the run. His muscular thighs pumped up and down, his feet digging into the sand as best they could to gain purchase for him to push off against. He'd made the error of wearing his baggy grey boxers for the run, proof that he wasn't thinking about what he was doing. He usually wore the tight black underwear, the ones that hugged him and cupped him and offered support where he needed it. On this run his package was belted by his inner-leg and he was sure he'd bruised his balls. Stupid fuckin' loose boxers! The burning in his lungs and legs was barely even registering in his brain, he was transfixed on the scenery.

The blue-green ocean with its cold appearance, looking like broken bottle glass. The white-brown sand, also looking so cold to his eye. The green hedges that ran along the top of the beach, separating the sand from the road and car parks. It was in one of those car parks that Billy had made his first "acquaintance" when he'd moved to the city. She was tall, maybe 5'9, had long black hair and emerald green eyes. She had a tight waist and a fully-developed bust. She had what the boys from the gym would call "bedroom eyes and blow-job lips." Her name was Sarah, or Samantha, or possibly even Rachel, something like that. She'd driven them out here to look at the moon and the way its reflection danced on the rippling black waves of the night sea.

As she'd spoken to him, some crap about how insignificant the moon made her feel, her hand had moved up his thigh, flattening the material of his black slacks, although at the crotch the material wasn't all that slack at all, and Billy had returned the favour by sliding his hand up her black stocking and under her black skirt, to find the warmth of her groin that was on fire with desire. He'd leaned over to kiss her, but missed her lips as she dove her face down towards Billy's hips. Her fingers artfully lowered his zip and Billy couldn't suppress a proud smile as she gasped when she took him in her hand. She brushed loose tassels of her hair behind her ear, smiled up at him.

'You should've told me about this sooner.'

Billy had tried to think of something clever to say, but his witticisms weren't an issue for too long, as she slid her moist, loving lips down over his tip, her head bobbing along in rhythm with song on the radio. What that song was, Billy couldn't, and never would remember. Funnily enough, he had other things on his mind. Her mouth moved further down his shaft with each bob, her soft hand cupping his ball and tickling them lightly with tender caresses.

Now as he slowed his run down, he was still noticing his surroundings. The birdless, ice-blue morning sky over-head was an endless landscape of possibility. Anything you could imagine could be up there. A person could envision a Biblical battle between the gods up there. Only nothing seemed to capture Billy's imagination for him to crack open the paints at home.

He cut his run short, a film of sweat forming on his waxy forehead and lining his upper-lip, the salt registering in his brain as the taste of exercise. He stood and watched the ocean lapping at the beach gently. He gazed out at the horizon and thought, What would Laurel make of all this? He told himself to go home, get showered and get to work. He was sure something would pop up, he just hoped it wouldn't be in the shower while he thought about Laurel.

CHAPTER THREE

Billy tried to come up with something exciting. Just create a pseudo-masterpiece, he thought. No problem. But then, he remembered, man does not create, he discovers. The tree came out looking like a large, up-right turd. The sunrise looked like a runny egg yoke that had been splattered after an egg was carelessly dropped from a great height. The pretty woman he attempted to commit to canvas resembled the Elephant Man. Even, as a last resort, when he attempted to paint a cute little kitten it resembled a bat that had been run over by a steam roller.

Paint the things you want to see. Well, what do I want to see? Billy thought for a while. What he'd really like to see was Denis, one of his fighters, winning the regional title tomorrow night. So, that's what he painted. He zoned out to some extent, not really being aware of what he was doing. The brush carried the paint to the blank surface that stared mockingly back at him, taunting him, daring him to create. The brush seemed to go wherever it felt like.

Three hours later, Billy couldn't believe it. He had painted a superb likeness of Denis, arm raised by a faceless old referee in a pale blue shirt, the championship belt wrapped snugly around the fighter's waist as though it was made specifically to be there. The opponent was reduced to a pair of boots and legs flat on the mat. Billy thought he could almost smell the sweat of the small arena. He could hear the crowd, some cheering but mostly booing. From the look of Denis in the painting, it must have been an early round knock out.

Monday night came. Denis got in the ring, had a frantic first-round exchange with both fighters trading punches, yet neither really getting the better of the exchanges. The pugilists muscles rippling down their arms and bodies, the strain etched out on their faces and sinewy chests. Sweat broke out on their shoulders and well-toned stomachs, making them gleam like Spartan sex machines ready for the very best type of action. In the second round, twenty-nine seconds in, Denis launched a huge right hook, that resulted in little over ten seconds later being crowned the new regional light heavyweight champion.

A loud chorus of boos rang out in the small boxing hall, as the now former champion who was taking an unexpected nap had chartered two coaches to bring some home-town support. A chill ran up Billy's spine breaking him out of goose-bumps all over his body, as the memory of the artistic endeavour the day before came back to him with the same force as Denis' right hook. The scene he had painted yesterday was now a living, breathing, sweating reality.

The events had unfolded as he had painted. The sun on Saturday. The boxing tonight. The possibilities of tomorrow.

***

Whilst everyone else had gone out for a few celebratory drinks after the show, Billy had gone straight home. Back in the locker room, as Denis was showering off what little sweat a few minutes work can bring, Billy had felt a pulse at the base of his penis. It was a weak pulse, more like a little twitch at first. He'd done hi best to ignore it, primarily by talking to Denis's family, his wife, or were they still not married just yet?, Jan, and the various promoters and guys from the gym.

Billy could feel the throbbing surge along his shaft and grow to a tingle as it reached the tip of his dick, he knew he was about to be overcome by sexual desire. He also knew that getting wood in a gym locker room when the only person who was naked was a flat-nosed brute of a man in the shower was a sure way to end a career.

He made his excuses and left, quickly. He ran home, it was only a fifteen minute sprint, and it did nothing to quell the desire burning in his groin. By the time he'd made it to his flat, got into the living room and got the TV on, his erection was borderline painful. He flicked the channels and found the one he was looking for, hoping for. A brunet with large, fake tits was bouncing up and down, kneeling on a pink-covered bed. She was holding a phone in her hand and waving it at the camera, enticing the horny, lonely viewers at home to call her. Billy dialled the number on screen quickly with one hand while trying to remove his clothes with the other-

'Fuck me!' he exclaimed upon seeing his twitching, hard cock, staring up at him. He was sure, certain that his manhood had never been so big. Stood there, with the faint voice of the TV station operator telling him he must be over the age of eighteen and have the bill-payer's permission to make this call, he started t understand why gay guys were gay. 'I'm getting turned on by my own stiffy,' he said absently to himself.

'Hi babes, what's your name?'

Holy shit, it's talking to me! The thought flashed briefly through Billy's mind before he realised that it wasn't his magical talking erection making the noise, but the busty brunet at the end of the line.

'Err, Willy,' Billy said, and slapped himself on the forehead. It was not the best cover name he could've used.

'Well hello, Willy. What have you been up to tonight?'

'Not much,' Billy said trying to stay calm, the phone in one hand, his shaft in the other. Don't rush this, keep it cool. Be calm. This thought sustained Billy over roughly twenty-seven seconds worth of conversation before he saw the price on the screen. Hurry it up, Bill, this call's costing too much to take it slow.

'Look, I'm not really used to this, but I've got a raging hard-on here and I need to blow my wad. Could you just talk dirty for a few minutes please?'

'Sure thing babes,' the busty brunet said, the smile was obvious in her voice, even if Billy hadn't been able to see it on his TV screen. 'What do you want me to say?'

'Well, uh, don't really know to be honest-'

'Want me to suck your big dick?' she interrupted.

'Yeah, yeah. Say that, that'll do it,' Billy agreed his excitement growing.

'I've never had one so big in my mouth before,' the busty brunet said over the phone. 'I hope I can fit it all in.'

And with that the busty brunet on the TV screen began to mock deep-throating the first two fingers on her hand, running her mouth up the side and then whirling her tongue around the tips. Billy's hand began to pump along the length of his sexual desire faster, faster, faster until his whole body began to move with the rhythm. The sweat slicked his palm and lubricated his cock making it glisten in the glow of the TV.

'I bet you would fill me up, babes. You'd have to be careful, one that size would hurt me, I've never taken a cock that fucking massive before, you big-dicked fucker! Fuck my pussy, fuck my pussy, fuuuuuuck, I'm so wet for you-'

Billy dropped the receiver from his head as he was overcome by a sudden orgasmic rush of fulfilment as he came. The power rushed from his legs and he fell to his knees, his thighs were very cold, and his length was bright red, sore-looking, and twitched slowly back down to normal size. The busty brunet on the screen looked up-set that her caller had suddenly disappeared from the end of the line. Billy searched the floor from where he knelt, but found nothing. Questioning his sanity, he got up and moved to the wall, found the switch and flicked the lights on. Eventually he found what he was looking for, seven feet from where he had been stood. Never, not once in all his years spent around macho men and their macho bullshit about sexual prowess, had he ever come across, pardon the pun, anyone who claimed to have shot their load seven feet across the room.

'Fuck...wow.' Billy turned the light in the living room off and went for a shower. He felt totally exhausted, and believed that once he climbed into bed he would sleep for an eternity.

***

Billy was sat outside at a table of a rather up-market little restaurant where he met with Denis now, to discuss some things over lunch. An expensive lunch. A champion's-pay expensive lunch. Billy was a apprehensive because at this low, regional level, even the title holders don't get paid that much. Denis was talking, but Billy had already that zoned out. He was scrunching up, then flattening out, just to scrunch up again a white napkin in his left hand.

'So what do you think?' Denis asked, expectantly.

'I'm sorry, what?'

'You never listen,' Denis continued. 'I was saying about me and Jan getting a house now. She's already three months gone, when can you line up another fight?'

'I don't know, Denis. I'm not really in at that end of it all.'

'Something on your mind, Billy?'

Billy was distracted. Across the street was a man with a small dog, a chihuahua. They were sat outside a coffee shop, one of the millions upon millions of coffee shops that had taken over the country and spread out like a cancer. Why on Earth would anyone living with this type of weather want to spend so much time outside?

Denis was talking again. Billy wasn't listening again. The man was being cruel to the dog, but Billy couldn't quite put his finger on how. He wasn't being physical or yelling at the poor pooch, but there was something. Just...something. Billy Found himself with a pen in his hand, doodling on the crumpled, creased napkin.

'So, do you think it's a good idea?' Denis posed the question.

'Sure.'

'Really?'

'No?'

'Yes or no, Billy? I really value your opinion. Should I buy a house or just stay in the flat?'

Billy thought it over for a moment, rolling the concept around in his head before adding, 'Buy the house, Den. Buy the house.'

Just then, from across the road outside the coffee shop, there was a blood-curdling scream. It was the man with the dog. The small chihuahua, with those enormous alien-like eyes, was chewing on what looked like a small piece of meat. The chihuahua had leapt up and bitten the owner in crotch, chomping off the man's left testicle, that it was now using as a punctured chew-toy.

'Wonder what's going on over there?' Denis said out loud to no one in particular as Billy looked down at the napkin on the table. He had sketched a perfect depiction of the small dog leaping though the air at its owner's groin. A cold sweat broke out on Billy's shoulders and chest. He could feel a tiny trickle run down his back. That was three things in a row that Billy had drawn and that had come to fruition. This could be very dangerous...or very rewarding.

CHAPTER FOUR

Billy spent the night awake, tossing and turning in his bed, throwing the covers about, the sheets resembling the mad waves of a frantic ocean storm. He was either too hot, at which point he'd shrug the sheets off his naked, sweat-slicked body, or he was too cold, when he'd pull the sheets onto himself and pull them snugly up to his chin. It was no good, he couldn't sleep. His skin was crawling with a million tiny invisible bugs. The pillow was damp from perspiration. His shoulders, arms and back itched incessantly.

He got up and showered, allowing the cool water to wash away the miniature bugs along with the soap suds. But still he could not sleep. He looked at the clock on his bed-side cabinet, his still blurry eyes told him it was three in the morning. Sleep was a small galaxy away from where he was now, and it wasn't going to get any closer on this night. Putting on some old jeans and an old denim shirt that he wore lopsided because he buttoned it up wrong, he made his way over to the easel and began to paint.

The brush moved about the page, the arm holding the brush felt weak but it moved quickly. The limb moved faster than Billy's brain could think. Again, Billy blanked out and lost all focus on the matter at hand. He placed the brush down and went to get an aspirin from the kitchen. His brain pounded inside his skull like a jack hammer, the worst headache he'd ever had the ill-luck of experiencing in his life.

Swallowing down the glass of cold water washed the two pills down his throat before they had a chance to leave a bitter residue on Billy's tongue (God how he hated that taste!), with it's bitter after-taste of iron and copper. Just to be safe, Billy chased another two pills down his gullet before returning to the painting.

Had he been carrying the glass of water at the time, he'd have dropped it shattering to the floor.

In the frame of the painting was the old bigot, Graham, from the art class. Flying through the air. A car was swerving across the street behind him. Billy had just painted the old bigot's death. The throbbing in Billy's brain had stopped now, the throbbing in his growing erection hadn't. A new pulsating took hold of his brain, how could he get to the old bigot and stop him getting hurt? Is it his place to stop the old bigot getting hit by the car? More tellingly, does he want to stop the old bigot Graham getting hit by that car, by any car?

One less bigot in the world. Would anyone care? Maybe the guy's family? He'd never spoken about any family, he probably doesn't see them anymore, and they probably like it that way.

Before Billy could come the any conclusion he passed out. A wave of black crashed over him and sent him spiralling to the floor. He awoke several hours later, just after nine that morning, with a large wet patch on the crotch of his old jeans. He wasn't able to take care of the built-up sexual desire, so his body had taken care of it for him. Billy couldn't remember in any real detail, but he had a nagging feeling that he'd dreamt of Laurel.

***

From that night until the following Saturday, Billy hadn't gone near a paint brush. He hadn't even looked at what little work he had done already, didn't even trust himself alone with a pen and a scrap of paper. Who knew what might happen?

It was a bright sunny Saturday, but not too bright. The type that makes you think you should get outside and do something even though you have no idea what exactly. It was sunny, but not too hot, it was what some would describe as comfortably warm. The sun didn't reflect too brightly off-white walls (when it did it blinded you), but the weather was nice enough to while away the hours in a beer garden, and not notice when the night crept in and it got chilly.

'Has anyone had any contact with...oh, what was his name?' Laurel asked the class bringing a hand up to her head as if to help her remember Graham's name. She was wearing a gorgeous white summer dress, that everyone noticed hugged and accentuated all the right places and curves. She looked angelically horny.

Her answer came by way of a class full of silent, slowly shaking heads. No one had seen him, no one had heard from him, and no one, except for Billy really cared what had happened to him.

After a brief moment of faux concern, the people in the class got down to painting. Today's object of artistic influence was a glass vase. Ever so slightly more challenging than a fruit bowl, but on par as far as excitement went. But Billy didn't want to paint the vase. He couldn't think of what he wanted to paint, but he damn-well knew it wasn't a glass vase. Maybe something beautiful? But what? He couldn't just start painting a portrait of

Laurel, that would be a little too obvious-

A little too obvious? He heard the Voice of Reason ask in his mind. You don't think painting a portrait of the woman might border on being extremely obvious?

And it was far too soon for Billy to start to committing Laurel's likeness to canvas anyway. They'd only known each other a week, not even that really, of Billy thought about it. There was the hour last week, during which they spoke for maybe five minutes, and now so far in this week's lesson they haven't said so much as hello to one another. So no, five minutes spaced out over seven days is not sufficient time to be painting portraits of a woman, no matter how deeply in lust with her you are.

But there was more to it than that, and Billy knew. No matter how hard he tried to deny it, no matter how much he silenced that nagging bitch in the back of his mind that was called the Voice of Reason, Billy was out-right afraid. Scared. Petrified to start painting. The moment the brush connected with the canvas (or the pen connected with the napkin or scrap of paper, for that matter) he lost all control and was possessed-

(Yes, the Voice of Reason told him, possessed is a good word for it, Bill.)

by some other force that he had no control over, and bad things happened as a result.

'Taking your time to get going?' Laurel's friendly voice snapped Billy back into reality like a bucket of ice-cold water in a drunkard's face. She was stood at his side, a huge smile on her face that was warm, comforting and gentle. It was the type of smile that made men weak at the knees and strong in the groin. And the really annoying thing, as far as the rest of the female population was concerned, was that it was perfectly natural. She'd never in her life spent time in front of a mirror when she was alone practicing a flirtatious smile, she'd never worried away the hours in a nervous panic about whether she was going to look good enough to attract the attention she wanted. She was the nicest person that other women would describe as 'bitch' anyone could ever hope to meet.

'It's just...' Billy searched for the right words. He couldn't remember the last time he'd been worried about not saying the right thing. 'It's not doing it for me.'

'I've never know anyone so fussy about what they're painting until after they've become famous,' she joked.

'You think I'll be famous?' he inquired, shooting back his own flirtatious smile. He felt foolish doing it, he wasn't really the flirting type, but Laurel appeared to be very receptive of the attention without intention.

'Why not?' she quizzed jovially. 'So, what are you going to paint today?'

'I don't know.'

'But not the vase?'

'Not the vase.'

'Ah well, I'm sure you'll think of something,' she said and placed her hand on his forearm. 'The Muse shall be upon you soon.'

She moved off around the rest of the class, passing the unmanned easel that Ol' Bigot Graham should have been stood behind. It was a huge, accusing tombstone looming over Billy. The easel knew. It knew that Billy held accurate information on the whereabouts of the Ol' Bigot. The large, ominous easel knew what Billy knew, it knew that Billy had caused it to happen.

It knew Billy had a dark secret, and it knew what it was.

Billy began to paint. He didn't bother with the background, as is the norm when painting, but just went straight into the main picture. It was Denis. He didn't see it at first, but the more paint he added-

(You mean that the forces possessing you force you to add)

to the page, the more colour he added to the portrait, the clearer the image became. Denis, wearing a dark suit. He was surrounded by gold circles. Coins! Billy thought, They're gold coins!

The thought made Billy smile. Denis was a good man, who needed money, and now. And now Billy-boy had just painted it. He hoped that good things would come of the-was it magic?-painting. The bad things came true, so maybe, just maybe if the world was fair-

(Which we all know it isn't, Billy-boy)

then maybe the good things will come true as well?

Denis with money. What a beautiful thought. That smile though. there was something about the way Denis was smiling that wasn't good, it didn't quite sit right with Billy. It wasn't the smile of a man who just won the lottery, that was for sure.

Laurel came over, the end of the class had yet again come without Billy noticing, and again, she stood looking on in amazement at the work of art Billy had been producing. It was so life-like, so vivid, so real.

'Well,' she began, 'it's certainly not the vase. Who is it?'

'His name's Denis. He's a boxer I coach.'

'Oh, you're a boxing coach. So you know how to handle yourself, then?'

Recently, Billy had been handling himself a lot more than usual, and Laurel's poor, or brilliant, choice of words brought a shy, child-like smile to his face. 'I do okay,' he replied. 'He's expecting a baby in a little while, and him and his missus are looking to buy a house. I'd really like to see him with some money.'

'Is he any good?'

'As a boxer, you mean?'

Laurel replied with a nod.

'He just became the regional light heavyweight champion.'

'He'll be rolling in it then.'

'Not quite. Only world champions make real money.'

'Well, even so, it's a nice thought.'

There was an awkward silence as both Billy and Laurel stared at the painting, occasionally shooting cheeky glances at each other out of the corner of their eyes. Laurel was running out of flirting options, just how many times was a girl supposed to squeeze a guy's arm before he got the message? Laurel wondered about why it was that Billy hadn't asked her out yet. She worried, briefly, that he might be gay, then dismissed this thought almost as soon as it came by telling herself that surely there were no gay men involved in boxing. She reminded herself to just be patient and keep flirting, and let nature take its course.

As if reading Laurel's thoughts, Billy told himself to just ask her out. One simple question to lead to one simple date to lead to one simple kiss to lead to one very complicated mess. He noticed her shuffle her feet where she stood, and he thought that the awkward silence had gone on too long.

'Oh well,' she said with a smile in her voice. 'I best be off. I'll see you next week.'

'Yeah,' Billy said almost vacantly. 'Yeah you will.'

Billy walked slowly out of the class and only when he reached the long hallway did he realise that he hadn't been able to smell the paints in the class. He didn't know if he did but just didn't notice them because he was now keeping paints in his home and had become desensitised to them, or if this was some side-affect of the possession that took place. All he really knew for sure was that he didn't much care, and would never care, just as long as nothing bad happened to Denis. He also noticed a warm sensation on his thigh, and realised that at some point along the way he had ejaculated. He was happy he was wearing black jeans, but he felt his cheeks getting warmer as he blushed and hoped that no one, especially Laurel, had been aware.

CHAPTER FIVE

Monday in the gym was a drag. All day Billy found it harder and harder to concentrate on the work at hand, his mind wondering away with itself. Thoughts of Denis and the money, and of Laurel, danced through his brain at every moment. A man who has much bigger men punching at his face can ill afford to suffer a lapse in concentration.

He hardly moved the focus pads at all, except for when his arms tired and he lowered them, but still only slightly. None of the young, hungry fighters he was coaching this day were getting all they could get out of him and their training time. the usual smell of fresh sweat on top of old sweat mixing in the atmosphere with the smell of old, worn leather gloves and pads was there, but only just, and nowhere near as strong as it could, and should, have been.

Distraught and distracted, Billy left early, instructing the few fighters who would still listen to him to do some work on the heavy bag for the remainder of the session. It was basic stuff, the type of thing people might learn in their very first boxing lesson, but it was sound advice and Billy could always get away with the excuse that once in a while it's good to go back over the basics to make sure you don't forget anything.

The closer he got to his home the stronger the smell of paints grew in his nostrils. Now he was worried. When he was miles away from any paints at all the smell was as strong and pungent as ever, but when he was locked in a warm room with them, he couldn't smell them at all. The stronger the smell got in his nostrils, the more powerful the throbbing in his head, and his penis, got. The headaches had become quite frequent as of late, which Billy had put down to being in a confined space with paint fumes and poor ventilation. The more frequent erections and sexual urges Billy had put down to, well, being a twenty-six-year old man who kept himself in pretty good condition.

But he was nowhere near the room in the apartment with the paintings now, he was a good few miles away from the paints and the brushes and the easels and the canvases, yet he could smell them so strongly it was almost overwhelming.

He crashed in through his front door, slamming it closed in his trail. He rushed his way to the small back room where he had set up his easel and paints, and quickly began preparing. He squirted paint from their tubes onto the pallet, dabbed his brush and began to bring colour and life to the blank white sheet. He had to get whatever this was over and done with quickly, because the erection in his shorts was threatening to rip out right through the material at any moment.

Once again time passed without Billy noticing. Again, Billy concentrated to the point where he zoned out. Again, Billy's headache, and groin ache, grew stronger and stronger and then subsided with a sudden pop, the urge washed away like foam from the shore, swept away with the next big wave of the tide.

The painting was finished.

He saw Laurel's face on the page staring back it him, surrounded by a pale, almost cold light. She was wearing a bright pink top and had a tender, flirtatious smile on her face. Billy thought she looked good enough to eat, which set his thoughts momentarily onto oral sex, how it would feel and taste and smell to have her silk-smooth thighs rubbing against his ears, and hooking themselves around the back of his neck. His horse-like erection came back instantly, and Billy knew before the hour was out he was going to have take care of it.

Turning his attention back to the painting he looked into the eyes on the portrait for what felt like a small eternity, imagining a friendly and jovial conversation. In the fantasy land in which the conversation took place, Billy had a witty, joking answer to everything Laurel said.

In the dream world of his fantasy, Billy had placed himself and Laurel in a bar made out of, or at least decorated, in bamboo.

They were on the beach of a tropical island paradise, miles from the hustle and bustle of other people. The only sounds were the gentle lapping of the ocean and the occasional squawk of pink parrots up in the lush, green trees. A welcome cool breeze drifted lazily through the open-plan bar, bringing Laurel's nipples to attention beneath her blue and green bikini top. She was wearing a green sarong that hugged and caressed her hips, the side of her tanned left thigh was visible and gave Billy ideas.

'It's nice here, isn't it?' she asked Billy in a husky voice that was designed to make him tingle in all the right places.

Billy's answer came in the form of action. He stepped forward and like the feeling of his hardness pressing against her as he kissed he passionately, their tongues darting about investigating each others mouths. His hands slid over her supple breasts and felt how her nipples had pebbled up because of the breeze. He kissed at her jaw-line and moved up her neck, finally coming to a stop on her ear, which he nibbled at excitedly.

Laurel pressed her body firmly against his, letting out soft, shallow, whispering groans into his ear. Her hands slid over his wide shoulders, across his thick, muscular chest and down his toned torso. Laurel's hands stopped at Billy's belt buckle, and undid it effortlessly. She slowly, but strongly groped at his growing manhood through the material of his shorts. Laurel broke their erotic embrace and smiled devilishly at Billy. To Billy the smile was mainly in her eyes, then she licked her lips.

She dropped to her knees and slowly dragged her finger nails up the outside of Billy's thighs, and then down the inside of them. In response to Billy's groans, Laurel asked him, 'You like that, don't you?', before pulling down his shorts and marvelling at his hard cock. Laurel leaned her face forward and gently covered the erection is small kisses, before taking him in her mouth and showing him what a real wild child can do when given some privacy.

Laurel stopped demonstrating her ability to suck a golf

ball through a garden hose, and climbed up on the wooden bar top, where she looked at Billy with an inviting twinkle in her eye, and pulled him to her using his dick as a handle.

Billy carefully spread Laurel's legs and kissed at her thighs before penetrating her with her fingers, holding her open as he moved his penis head closer to her waiting pink mouth-

A thought came to Billy just then that brought him back to the sterile reality of the real world. Pink. How exactly had he been able to paint Laurel wearing a pink top when all he had were the primary colours? You could mix red, blue and yellow anyway you like but you'd never in a million years come up with pink. Red and blue gives you purple, red and yellow gives you orange. Add some blue to yellow and get green. He would need to add white to the red to get pink, but he didn't have white. Billy felt a shiver run up his spine and he shuddered uncontrollably. He forced himself to look down at the pallet, afraid of what he might find there, but needing to make certain that he didn't have a white paint globule there.

He didn't.

He did, however, find tiny droplets of red, much more watery than the red paint, and much richer, much brighter. As he looked down at the tiny droplets, they were joined by another. Then another.

Billy's nose had begun to bleed.

The flat felt small and stuffy, suffocating him. The air was too hot to breath and was sure the walls were closing in around him. He picked his jacket up off the floor where it had fallen, landed, when Billy flung it off as he entered his home, and left. He decided he just needed to spend a little bit of time in an open space, yet indoors. Where there were people about, but not too many, who would leave you alone. Billy headed for the 24 hour super grocery store.

***

Buzzing. Billy was sure he could hear the yellow neon lights in the white ceiling buzzing like incessant flies. Buzzing with a power, a surge, a life force. He pushed the cart around the aisles, as he had done for the last fifteen minutes, and it was still empty. The old adage was never shop for food when you're hungry, you only end up buying a bunch of junk you don't really need, or truly want. Now, Billy was facing a problem of the polar opposite; he wasn't at all hungry and didn't find any of the food appetising and was seriously doubting if he'd ever eat again-

(We both know what you'd like to eat though, don't we?)

Billy was having more and more trouble controlling that voice in the back of his mind, the voice he felt he'd made a mammoth mistake naming the Voice of Reason. He stopped walking a moment to clear his head, to shut that voice up.

(You'd love to taste her, right now, right here. You'd love to have your face buried deep inside her, licking every single centimetre of her body, plunging deep into her-)

Billy slapped himself, hard, across the face, leaving the faint red outline of his own hand on his cheek. He had to control his mind, because those types of thoughts were making him aroused, and walking around the supermarket with a giant hard-on was not the way to make friends. Well, not the right type of friends, anyway. He pushed his cart on down the aisle when another thought hit him, Why do I always get the one with the wobbly wheel?

He pushed the still-empty shopping cart with the wobbly wheel to the end of the aisle of frozen food and, clunk!, straight into the front of a cart coming the other way out of the next aisle over.

'Oops,' Billy said as the impact reverberated through his wrists and up his forearms. 'Didn't see you there.'

'It's okay,' the familiar voice replied. 'I didn't se you either.'

Billy looked up at the 'driver' of the other cart and saw the same pretty eyes and flirtatious smile as he had painted earlier in his apartment before fleeing that stuffy place. He quickly remembered the lights in the background of the painting looked cold. Billy and Laurel were now standing in the frozen food section.

'So what's a talented guy like you doing in a place like this at this unearthly hour of the morning?'

Billy hadn't realised it, but it was now quarter past one in the morning.

'I, uh,' Billy began, struggling as he was to find the right words. 'I'm shopping.'

Peering into his cart, Laurel told him, 'You could've fooled me,' and flashed that ever-increasingly sexy and inviting smile at him. It felt as though that smile was just for him.

'I'm not feeling overly hungry at the moment.'

'Aren't you planning on being hungry later on?'

'Does anyone ever plan on being hungry?'

'Oh, snap!' Laurel said as her smile broke into a tiny laugh. She was stroking Billy's biceps as she did.

This is it Billy-boy, he told himself. And even if she says no, you can just go home and paint it.

(And jerk yourself into a coma)

'Erm,' Billy said nervously. 'Do you want to go and get some food tomorrow?'

'I'm getting food now.'

'No, I mean like, where it's already cooked.'

'You mean a date?

'Well you can eat what you want.'

'Oh, aren't we the funny man?'

Billy smiled. It was half nervous and half almost borderline confident.

'Is that a yes?'

'Suppose so,' Laurel grinned, pulling her shoulders back forcing her breasts out. 'Where are you taking me?'

(Right here you horny bitch-)

'Don't know, where would you like to go?'

'Anywhere is fine. Do you know of anywhere?'

'I know lots of places, but none are suitable for a lady.'

'A lady? Oh, I like the sound of that.'

And so the conversation went on, with both trying to out-flirt the other, as they wondered aimlessly through the aisles. At some point Billy started to absent-mindedly place items into the cart. Somewhere along the line, Laurel began adding items to Billy's cart, too.

<u>CHAPTER SIX</u>

It was early morning. The roads were slicked with ice, and an eerie white mist crept along, standing three feet off the ground. Her weary eyes were blood shot and tired, the effects of the coffee she'd had an hour earlier had already worn off. By all-rights, she should've pulled over to a lay-by, locked the doors and had herself a few hours of deep, much-needed, sleep.

But she didn't.

And when the car lost traction on the road, she was unable to wrestle it back.

At just after six AM, Denis, still fast asleep, and alone in his bed, became a widower.

***

Denis's all-black suit looked smart, but it was his mother who had to iron his white shirt for him.

Denis was left without a wife.

Denis was left with the knowledge that his unborn child had died in the womb.

Denis got his cash, though. Quite a tidy sum paid out through his deceased wife's life insurance.

It was not the way Billy wanted Denis to get the cash.

CHAPTER SEVEN

The next morning when Billy woke, he was...what was that feeling? He felt like his whole body was feather-light, totally relaxed at all his limbs. Except for his stomach. His stomach was hollow, save for the mass of butterflies fluttering about in there in anticipation of the date with Laurel. He'd spent some time when he'd gotten home working a shine onto his dress shoes and ironed a dark blue shirt. He was giddy.

For the first time in a long while, Billy felt at peace.

He couldn't really say he'd dated much in the past few years, and he was quite worried about the womanly effect that had been plaguing his mind, What will I wear? Will that look good? Oh God, what if we clash?

With a deep breath, the headache came on, but not as powerfully as previous bouts. What did come on stronger than before was Billy's all-consuming urge to release some sexual tension. Had he dreamt of Laurel last night? He couldn't remember very clearly, but he was sure he had done. He must have done. Billy made quick work of the morning glory in the bathroom as he thought of Laurel (and the actress Krista Allen, well the more the merrier). After taking care of business, Billy downed three aspirin for the headache and began opening all of the windows of his second floor apartment. The room he went to last was the small back room where he kept all of his painting equipment. He stood in the doorway, almost afraid to enter the room itself.

There was a power to the room. He could feel that now. Not necessarily evil, but a force so strong that it scared Billy. It terrified him. It was a force that seemingly answered to no one. It did what it wanted, whether it fell on the side of good or right was apparently immaterial to it. Billy thought it was much like a gun in some respects. It was a very dangerous thing, it could be extremely dangerous in the wrong hands, even if they do happen to be well-meaning hands. Even the best of men sometimes do bad things.

Forcing himself to enter Billy crossed the small room on legs made of jello carrying feet made of concrete. He opened the window and inhaled the fresh (if it could be called fresh) air from outside in an attempt to calm himself. The headache, still in its foetal stage, was gnawing at Billy's brain like a rat chewing at the tail end of an old curtain. For a fleeting moment Billy wondered if this room was haunted. Nah, he told himself, it's more likely you've developed a brain tumour. This produced a healthy, but sad, little chuckle from Billy.

Turning to cross the room back to the door he noticed a brush had fallen to the floor. Must've rolled off the table, he surmised as he bent down to pick it up. Then, as if no-longer under his control, the brush dipped into a fresh dollop of paint on the pallet and began to spread the colour on the easel.

'No,' Billy attempted to say in defiance, but it was no use. He was painting. The small headache completely disappeared. He knew it had absolutely nothing to do with the pills he'd taken a few minutes earlier. He also knew that the thought of Krista Allen and Laurel rolling around on satin sheets was not the reason his erection was back with a vengeance. The work was quick-paced, the arm moving furiously. Billy had zoned out, but he was dimly aware of his shoulder to get hot, to burn with a fiery ache.

At last, he found his way through a milky-white fog and snapped to, suddenly back in reality with a start, the jump sending little flicks of red off the brush onto the fresh painting.

The painting.

It looked like a building in mid-explosion. The flames grew

high and licked at the sky. It wasn't a tall building, maybe two floors, and grey. Billy thought he could see tiny fragments of glass in the flames, where the windows would have blown out, he supposed. What building it actually was, Billy couldn't quite work out.

The explosion he'd painted seemed controlled, if such a thing can really exist. It wasn't an accident, that was the vibe the painting was giving off. Billy got the impression that the disaster was predetermined, someone had had planned the explosion. He felt a warm trickle of sweat slowly creeping its way down his bare, muscular chest. It was only when he glanced down to look at the sweat he noticed his raging erection poking up. It was then that he became all-consumed by the desire to procreate. If Laurel had been there with him at that moment she would not have been safe. He would have liked to have-

(Eat her out! Fuck her senseless! Make her scream your name loud enough to wake the dead! Make her thankful to any and all gods that she was born a woman!)

Billy dropped his shorts and began to pleasure himself, he was sure that he'd never felt his erection be so hard, so solid, in all his life. The waves of pleasure built as they pulsed through his cock, finally the pressure building to be too much to contain. He came powerfully, feeling as though something large had just been dragged out of his body through his penis. It was a good feeling that left Billy much calmer, much more serene. Whatever it was that had caused the monumental build-up had dissipated, for now at least. Catching his breath and gathering his thoughts, Billy made a mental note to think about what brought it on. Why was it that every time he painted he felt the urge to defile a beautiful woman, and why is causing such headaches?

Billy got cleaned up (and wiped the painting and the easel clean after they got caught in the flight path of Billy's sex-shot), and then spent the day putting together a decent-looking first date outfit for later that evening. Most of his clothes were what he called 'gym clothes,' meaning they were loose and informal and had that scent of old sweat, like old, warm ham, that clung to every fibre. The good clothes he had were used for special occasions only, like photo opportunities or fighter's court appearances.

The dark blue shirt and shined-up shoes he'd prepared he now worried would look a little too formal. 'Hell with it,' Billy decided and went into town to get himself some new clothes. Buying new clothes just for the sake of one date? You really are turning into a woman there, Billy-boy.

***

All the while he was shopping (a day's events that lead to the purchase of a black pair of trousers, a sand-coloured pair of trousers, a light blue shirt and a dark red shirt) he racked his brain trying to figure out just what the building was that he had painted. A bank? A shop? Offices? A bar? A library? he was never going to figure it out, at least not when he was stuck in the heaving throng of shoppers. Billy thought about that and asked himself, who are all these people? Shouldn't they be at work?

Billy didn't like people, not in masses. People were foolish, they reacted stupidly, they'd panic over the dumbest things. They'd push and cram and get silly with each other when queuing, or they'd make strange grumbling noises under their breath. Then someone would get to their breaking point and then the trouble starts. Billy would always make sure to get whatever little Christmas shopping he had to do done by the end of October.

What building was it? Billy thought that perhaps it wasn't even a building in this city, or country for that matter. There was no saying the events of the painting would actually come true. There was no saying the that what occurred in the painting would even take place this week, it might be way off in the future. Just don't think about it, he told himself. Put it out of your mind. Concentrate on the date. Yes.

The date that he hoped would go well but knew in his heart would go very badly. How else could it go? She was a very beautiful, sexy lady, who was obviously fairly intelligent and would have been on more than her fair share of dates. Or at the very least she'd have had her share of suitors. Comparing this to his own life Billy felt depressed. His own life was spent around aggressive men. He wasn't sure he'd know how to be around a very attractive woman without some type of buffer zone.

Forget about it, he advised himself. If it all goes to Hell, which it will then it all goes to Hell. Nothing you can do about that, Billy-boy.

He went home, and practiced conversations out loud with himself, hoping that he was just nervous, and that he wasn't actually going insane. He was also hoping that none of his neighbours could hear him. Holding the light blue short in one hand and the recently ironed dark blue shirt in the other hand, Billy asked himself, what are some good things to talk about? Um…okay, never mind, what are some bad things to talk about on a first date with a woman who's totally out of your league?

'Boxing,' Billy said to himself. 'Just steer clear of it, and everything associated with it. Violence in general, actually. Just don't mention it. Painting! Painting? No, it's too 'work-related' for her. Also don't mention anything that's really quite boring and was only made to be used as small-talk.'

Now Billy-boy, just so you know this includes MDF, vinyl underwear, animals, trash bags, the prices of things these days, politicians, sex, religion, wallpaper, wicker, salt shakers, place mats, candles, wax, funny shaped ears, ear wax, arm-pit hair, baldness, cardigans, body odour, the list goes on, Billy-boy, that list goes on.

Remember one simple rule; let her do the majority of the talking. Let her choose the subject matter, and let her do most of the talking.

He showered and found the fruit scents of the body wash

to be relaxing, even though it made his skin tingle. Most people assumed that men only ever purchased the most basic of shower gels, but Billy had been buying the kind that had scrubbed the skin almost raw for years. It was the only way to really get the smell of the gym off him at the end of the day. The shampoo he used smelled strongly of mint, and the conditioner smelled like coconuts (admittedly, Billy had picked up the wrong bottle and then not had the guts to put it back when he got to the check-out and realised his mistake). He brushed his teeth, shaved very carefully (tonight was not the night to cut himself) and applied just a dab or two of aftershave. Billy looked at the bottle and lamented. They don't call it aftershave anymore, they call it a fragrance. Used to be aftershave, then it was cologne, which was just barely passable, but now it had evolved into fragrance. When he was a small child it was called very masculine things like Hi Karate. Karate. We called it after a martial art, the style of killing a person with an empty hand. Now they're called things like Phoo-Phoo-de-Poo. They used to come in manly bottles, now they come in metal balls. Billy was sure there was a metaphor in there somewhere.

He checked himself in the mirror before leaving the apartment. There was no full-length mirror in the apartment, how he looked had never really been of any importance to him before now. If the world didn't like the way he looked well then the world was invited to just go screw itself sideways! But now? Now was different. Now was the chance to impress a beautiful woman, now was the chance to show that he was more than just a grunt with a flair for artistry. Now was a chance to show he could function as a normal member of society.

This is your chance, Billy-boy. Don't blow it.

CHAPTER EIGHT

The restaurant reeked of cash. It was soaked in high-price cologne and nasty-smelling perfume that you just knew came with an even nastier price tag. Big-nosed men in fancy suits sat with women that were young enough to be their daughters but were more likely upper-class escorts. Hookers who accept credit cards, as they were known to most.

Everything was white in the restaurant, the ceilings, the walls, the tablecloths. The chandeliers were faux-gold fixtures with glass pretending to be crystal hanging down like expansive tear drops. The menus were red-brown leather with Marella's scrawled across it in gold lettering. It was a place to be seen. It was a status symbol to eat there.

Billy's nervousness turned to juvenile laughter that he tried to stifle somewhat unsuccessfully as he and Laurel were shown to their table. Yes, it was quite true that he was not in the business of high finance, nor was he ever going to be the type of person who spent hours checking the stocks and shares in the newspapers. However, he had a half-ownership deal on a gym two cities over, had coached no-less than seven boxers of varying weight classes to at the very least regional titles, and had been a personal fitness trainer since he was nineteen. His accommodation was modest to say the least, his car (if the rust bucket could really still be called a car) was almost as old as he was. He didn't have any vices, such as booze, drugs or video games.

Essentially Billy worked long hours for decent enough pay and very rarely spent a penny of it. He was, as the hip cats might have said, loaded.

Laurel, by the way, looked amazing. When Billy picked her up in The Junkie (that was what he'd nicknamed the car, even though it wasn't a name he shared with people too often), his immediate reaction had been to just reach out and grab Laurel and hug her closely and kiss her madly. She was wearing a very elegant green evening gown, and her eyes were the sexiest damn things Billy had ever seen. They were bright white things lined by a thin black circle. Billy would have married her right there and then. Of course, every other woman they had passed would have liked to have killed Laurel for looking so good, right there and then.

The big-nosed snooty man in the blue suit led them to their table and gave Billy and dirty look when he pulled the chair out for Laurel. Evidentially, the usual rich snobs who came in here didn't help their upper-class hookers to sit down.

'Oh, thank you,' Laurel said with a trace of surprise in her voice. 'Aren't you just the gentleman?'

'M'lady,' Billy joked.

Snooty Nose went back to the main doors to resume host duty.

'This is a very nice place,' Laurel said in a slightly hushed tone as she glanced about the place taking it all in. 'Feel a little out of my depth.'

'Really? Why?'

'Don't know, I'm just not used to going to such nice places.'

Laurel smiled at him with those perfect lips and snow-white teeth. Her hair was up showing off the sexiest, most slender neck he'd ever seen that didn't belong to some cartoon woman drawn by some horny Japanese teen.

Any minute now Billy-boy, you're going to say something that's going to destroy the evening. She'll run out, and the whole building is just gonna turn around and stare at you accusingly. You'll be able to hear them, whispering to each other, "I bet he propositioned her!", "You know what I think? I think he proposi-tioned her and when she said no he insulted her, that's what I think" Hey Billy-boy, I really think you should be paying atten-tion to her right now.

'Don't you?'

Her question hung in the air, waiting for an answer that was never going to come.

'Sorry?' Bill asked shaking his head slowly and blinking. Luckily for him, Laurel giggled. 'I'm really sorry, I zoned out.'

'Sorry, was that?' she asked, smiling and leaning forward to touch his arm. 'I was just asking what you think about these people over here. I don't think she's his daughter, do you?'

'Erm,' Billy began tentatively. 'To be honest with you, Laurel, I'm pretty sure you're the only woman in here who's not being paid to be.'

'What, all of them?'

'Well, let's see. Most of the women in here are definitely on the job, and the other women are the staff, so...yeah.'

'On the job?'

'What?'

'I love it when you talk rough.'

A red hue came over Billy's face as the blood rushed to his cheeks (a welcome departure from his blood rushing elsewhere) giving them a rosy blush. Laurel noticed this, how could she not?, and let out a cheeky giggle at the idea of grown man blush like a child.

'My God,' she said laughing with, not at, Billy. 'Are you blushing?'

'No, no,' Billy lied. 'It's just the heat and the wine.'

'We haven't had any wine.'

'Probably just the heat then.'

They shared a silent smile before Laurel added, 'Can't imagine what you must've been like in school.'

'Yeah, well, in school...' Slowly it dawned on Billy. 'School...'

'What about it? Laurel asked. 'Are you okay?'

'School...erm, I'm fine, fine...would you excuse me for a minute please?'

Billy was up and out of his chair before his words had a

chance to register in Laurel's perfect, yet pixie-like ears. She was left somewhat in a state of confusion as she watched the empty chair before her sit motionless as the blue streak of Billy's shirt darted across the room to the maitre-dee who pointed Billy over to a quiet hallway behind a wall on the way to the kitchen.

The pay phone was stoic, a blank face stared back at Billy for some time in the black shine of the smooth receiver. At last he plucked up the courage and lifted the receiver to his ear. He dialled the number and dropped the coin, which fell noisily back out of the machine on the coin tray. It was then that Billy remembered a person doesn't get charged for calls to the emergency services.

With a click the nasally voice came through the receiver into Billy's ear.

'Emergency services-'

'Police, please,' Billy cut the woman off.

'Where are you sir?'

'What's that matter?' Billy asked in a panic, sweat getting heavier in his forehead.

'I need to know your location to know which police station to put you through to, sir.'

Wiping the sweat from his eyebrows with his fingers, Billy gave over the details of the city he was in and that this was very, very urgent, please hurry.

'All calls to the emergency services are urgent, sir.'

'Really? You think now is the time to get attitude?'

A series of clicks and eventually Billy was put through to someone on a reception desk who sounded like a gruff old lady coming to the end of a particularly long, and stressful, day. Billy momentarily wondered what would happen if someone were in real trouble here, and time was of the essence? What if someone was getting mugged or killed and it was extremely urgent?

He explained that it was his belief (is my name really important?) that someone was going to (no it's not someone I know) try to blow up a school (no I'm not going to give you my name) somewhere in the city. So many questions were asked by the old bothersome battle-axe at the other end that Billy was forced to ask her if she got everything he'd told her.

A school. A fucking school! What kind of maniac would want to blow up a school? Maybe it was an accident (Billy hoped it was, there was something very disturbing about the thought that someone would purposefully blow up a school)? Maybe it was just a gas leak or something and somebody flicked a light switch and that sparked the explosion? Screw it, it was too late to go back now , he told himself. He'd made the call, given what information he himself had, and that was all there was to it.

Placing the receiver back down on the phone he cut the other voice off mid-sentence. The sweat had matted down his hair at the temples and Billy decided to take a trip to the gents after taking in several long, deep breaths. What if the police traced the call? Was he on camera? Would he get into trouble for that phone call? Had he done anything to get in trouble for? Well, yes. If it turned out nothing was wrong he could be arrested for wasting police time. If something did happen, then how exactly did he know about it?

Well officer, I knew something was going to happen because I had a blackout and then I painted this psychic picture. Oh, and it also causes me to have very bad head aches and an insatiable appetite for this blond woman I know.

What would be worse, if they didn't believe him or if they did?

The cold water from the faucet in the men's room swelled around the basin with a ferocious power, as Billy cupped his hands together and splashed the cool wetness into his face. The bathroom was all bright white marble with gold veins. The taps were gold fish. The water shot out of their mouths. Billy felt sick, though he wasn't sure if that was brought on by the events of the last few minutes or the vomit-inducing decor he was surrounded by.

Well done, Billy-boy. You've managed to make yourself nauseous in a very expensive, high-class restaurant. Remember that you're here on a date and, you know, might want to get back to her.

Billy made his way back to over to the table where he was surprised to see Laurel was still sat. He was also quite taken aback by the fact that her eyes got wider and her face cracked a smile as he returned.

'Sorry about that,' he said sitting down. 'I just had to make a phone call. Sorry.'

'It's okay. Important?'

'Very, yes.' Then he quickly added, 'How could it not be to drag me away from you?'

'Creep,' she smiled with a flutter of her eyelashes. 'I didn't say stop.'

'What do you want?' Billy lightly head-butted the menu he held in front of him. 'I mean, what do you think you'll have?'

'You're cute when you worry about offending me.'

A waiter came over with a small note pad in his hand and an air of either confidence or arrogance, Billy couldn't quite make out which.

'Are you ready to order?' The waiter asked, his attention momentarily drifting away from the matter at hand and over to Laurel's tanned cleavage. He did a poor job of hiding his wondering glance, and it was only that Laurel had her head in the menu that she didn't see.

'Err,' Billy hated indecisiveness in his voice. 'What do you suggest?'

'I suggest, sir,' the waiter began, 'that you turn your menu the right way up.'

A hush fell over the table. Laurel hid the lower part of her face behind the menu, her cheeks raised up and creased reached out from the outer corners of her eyes, letting Billy know she was smiling. She resisted the urge to say, 'Oh bless.'

'Do you have anything with chicken?' Billy asked flatly.

'Several dishes, sir,' the waiter was adding just the right amount of emphasis on the word sir to make Billy want to punch the man, hard, in the groin. 'We have-'

'Bring me one,' Billy interrupted.

'I see. And for the lady?'

***

The date went as well as could be expected, Billy's mind occasionally slipping back to the school, and the explosion, and the idiots that were on the other end of the phone. It turned out that Laurel came from a very happy family, she had a sister (hello!) who she hadn't seen in a while, not since the wedding-

(Whose?)

(The sister's.)

(Oh good.)

And she went to college, and then to university to study art. Painting, sketches, even a part-time fling with wedding photography at one point.

'And what about you, Billy?'

He explained that he had begun boxing when he was eight, when a long-forgotten relative had bought him a pair of boxing gloves for Christmas. From there he began training properly, moving up the amateur ranks and winning a lot more than he lost. He studied sport science (not the contradiction in terms that people thought it was) and became a fully qualified and certified fitness instructor with the YMCA not long after. He felt a calling towards coaching boxing more than he ever did actually competing, and turned people's careers around. In the last ten years his own in-ring record was the not-so-impressive 7-0.

A few hours later and the bill was paid and Laurel was stood at the front door of her apartment building.

'I um, I had a really good time tonight, Billy.'

'I'm glad, me too.'

She looked around nervously, an awkward silence falling between them. Neither was too sure what they should do or say, or if they should do or say anything at all. They certainly didn't want to talk to just to say something and say the wrong thing.

'Erm, do you want to do this again?' Billy asked, doing a terrible job of hiding his nervousness.

'What, talk to you?' she asked playfully. 'Yeah, I do.'

'No, I meant, like, see each other, type of...thing.'

Laurel placed her hand on the side of his face, and smiled. 'God, you're so bad at this. Good job that you're really cute when you're nervous.'

She moved forward, tilted her head and kissed him. It was a hell of a kiss. Billy was expecting maybe a friendly peck on the cheek, even if it was just a thanks for the meal kiss, but this? This was way beyond anything Billy was hoping for. He brought his hands up to the sides of her head and ran his fingers through her long blond hair. He really hoped she wasn't offended by his raging hard-on that was prodding her in the thigh.

The kiss was having an effect on Laurel, too. She experienced the after-taste of the sauce Billy's chicken had been cooked in, could almost taste the aroma of the meal. She could also feel her crotch getting warmer as the blood rushed there, and the bulge she felt coming from Billy's groin didn't nothing at all to calm her down.

They parted lips but their eyes remained closed for a short

spell afterwards. The pulled their heads back and smiled, slightly embarrassed, both of them, and they felt ashamed and shy. Billy felt somewhat exposed, but that was largely due to his pointing the way, even though both hands still cupped Laurel's face.

Finally composing herself enough to speak she told Billy, 'You can call me tomorrow, if you want.'

'What's wrong with just calling you Laurel?'

'Oh, confident enough to make jokes now, are we?'

'Yeah...yeah I am,' Billy said with a smirk. 'It's funny how little things can boost your confidence.'

'Little?' she pressed up against him.

Billy broke into an embarrassed, nervous laughter as Laurel watched his face intently. She really found him quite attractive, and the more he blushed and shied away from compliments, the more she found herself drawn to him. She could see that Billy was a very intelligent man, just maybe not the most articulate person. Just because he found it hard to express his thoughts and feelings didn't mean he didn't have them.

'I'll call you tomorrow,' he told her.

'You better.'

'I will.'

They looked at each other for a long, drawn-out moment, maintaining eye contact, before his smile broadened and he leant in to kiss her again. After yet another bout of tongue wrestling, she informed him, 'I really have to go in now.'

CHAPTER NINE

All the way home Billy had a slightly moronic smile on his face, the type that no amount of dissecting the nights events could remove. He was, he believed, happy. He had managed to go out, actually out of the house for a trip that didn't involve going to the gym, and managed to function in society. He had taken out a beautiful, and amazingly beautiful, young woman to dinner, and it had gone well, very well, he thought. What had she made of the mysterious phone call, though? Had she thought there was another woman on the go? No, not very likely. Laurel didn't strike Billy as the type of woman that would stay on a date, and then instigate a passionate kiss, if there was another woman in the picture.

Just don't dwell on it, you dumb-ass, he told himself. Just be glad that she seemed to enjoy herself ('She clearly did' he said out-loud) so just be happy with that. It was more than you were hoping for, and more than you deserve. And for the love of every-thing nice and sweet and good and happy in your life, do not for-get to call her tomorrow.

***

The bedroom was humid, the sweat dampening his pillow and the sheet beneath him absorbing mush of the sweat that was seeping out of his tense, powerful back. He rose, wiped his eyes even though sleep had at no time taken him, and got up. He moved to the kitchen without turning on any of the lights, the bright beam emitted from the refrigerator hurt his eyes, causing him to wince. The brightness forced a painful pressure up to the front of his head.

He took a carton of milk and closed the door, letting the kitchen fall back into darkness again. He searched for a glass for a brief moment before deciding to just guzzle the milk from the carton regardless, a practice he hadn't performed since he was eleven years old. The headache brought on by the refrigerator lights hadn't dissipated, but his mind was drawn to the dull ache in his belly where the cold milk had hit in abundance with a ven-geance.

Billy put the milk back, this time shielding his eyes from the harsh light, and made his way back to the bedroom. Only upon closing the bedroom door did he feel something was very wrong. He had that gnawing energy that could only, and would only be burned up by a carnal act. Everyman on the planet past a certain age knows it, and most "respectable" women past that same age deny it exists for them. If there was so much as even late-night soft-core porn on the TV that would do. There was something else too. The room felt claustrophobic to him. It seemed too small in the dark silence.

There was something not quite right.

Sensing something was wrong, Billy reached for the light switch with his right hand. He could feel nothing but the cold wallpaper beneath his open palm. He stretched his left hand into the silent, motionless darkness, and he knew what he would feel. There it was, the light switch on the wall. Even before he flicked the switch he knew what he would see.

The switch was flicked.

The lightly dusted bulb hanging bare from the ceiling blinked into life and lit up the room.

The easel stood side-on in front of Billy.

He moved around the easel and stood in front of it now, staring at the painting of the exploding school. The erection flared up and pulsated, making his cock bounce rhythmically. It was sending shooting, stabbing pains to his balls, begging to be taken care of and soon. This made Billy roar and twitch in sudden movements like a giant, randy fish out of water, the need, that urge, causing his body to twist and turn and contort into odd, doubled-over shapes. The churning in his stomach was completely forgotten about. The pain-like sensation began to pound along with electric bolts that shot through his whole reproductive system.

He could visualise millions and millions of ferocious little sperms with razor-blade teeth snapping granite jaws at his insides.

The pounding and pulsating grew stronger and stronger, it's power growing with each throb. His torso was covered in a coat of sweat, as was his manhood, which glistened in what little light was entering the room.

In his right hand he held a paint brush, in his left he held his hard cock. He painted frantically, he masturbated furiously. Was he still enjoying the sensation? He couldn't tell. He just knew that he had to get whatever it was inside him out as soon as he could. His right hand swooped and swooshed over the page, his left hand pumped back and forth, closer to and then further away from his body. When his penis shot forth the first massive load, Billy didn't notice. He kept on jerking away, never allowing his erection the chance to wind down. He kept going.

After seven hours (although Billy had lost all track of time) of frantic painting and self-love, something inside Billy's head snapped, making him drop the brush to the floor which he collapsed next to in an unconscious heap. His seed that had splattered the room began to congeal. The paints that had splattered around the room began to harden and crust. He lay on the floor in a crumpled mound, limbs bent under his torso, his head cocked to one side, a small trail of saliva crept from his mouth.

The sun rose higher and higher in the sky, it peeked high in the sky at midday, and then began its arch downwards. At just after two in the afternoon, the light began to back room where Billy kept his easel and was now sleeping on the floor, shaped like a naked human pretzel. The sunlight burned bright orange through his thin eyelids, sending little dots dancing in front of his eyes.

He awoke with the sun glaring in his eyes, dried semen on his belly and right thigh, and a dirty-feeling layer of dried sweat everywhere else. He felt grubby. His limbs and neck felt very sore where he'd slept funny, and there was a large bump on the back of his head which he'd banged when he passed out and collapsed.

'What? Why?' his throat was sliced from inside by a million tiny razors when he spoke, the symptoms of a sore throat brought on by breathing through the mouth in a cold room all night.

Standing up, his left arm cocked behind his head feeling the bruised bump, his vision (complete with dancing dark spots) fell on the easel. The exploding school had been painted over. In its place was now a police-controlled crime scene. A collection of cars parked in a semi-circle. Several police officers with their guns drawn and a man lying face-down on the concrete. Small trickles of blood ran from his body. A single blood creek ran from his head. The school building in the background was completely undamaged.

A painful smile spread on Billy's face.

Billy showered and shaved, at various times battling wooziness and losing his balance, wondering what he was going to eat. He knew he had to eat something, he'd lost a lot of 'energy' judging from the state of his legs and the dull-ache of his left arm, only nothing he could think of was appealing to him. The thought of food turned his stomach. Light-headedness came in waves, forcing Billy to cut his usually short shower even shorter. It would be a hell of a thing to survive dropping like that and getting the bump on the head, just to then fall in the shower and drown to death.

(But what a clean, nice-smelling corpse you'd leave behind!)

***

The man had been a good family man once upon a time. But, at some point since his son was born four years ago, the death of his mother had taken its toll. During the first few months after her death, the marriage to hi wonderful wife had become strained and stressed, and in his eyes, the Wife was never as kind or caring or loving as Mother had been. They grew apart quickly and filed for a divorce that came in no time. Due to the extended grieving and refusal to get over the death, the man had lost his job, which in turn led to him losing his home and forced him to live in a hovel, not much more than a hole in a wall. No job and crummy living quarters made it exceptionally easy for his ex-wife to get full custody of their son.

Their four year old son went to school in a small grey building. When the police had found the man after being tipped off by an anonymous caller the night before, he had his passport in his coat pocket, six hundred dollars in bills in his wallet, and several kilograms of semtex strapped to his stomach. He'd reached into his coat to retrieve a picture of himself, his ex-wife and their son on his very first Christmas (the little boy didn't really have a clue what was going on and was frankly terrified by Santa). The police thought he was going for some kind of detonator.

The bullets ripped through the man's body easily and quickly, the swift efficiency puncturing organs and muscles. The one shot that penetrated the man's skull stopped everything.

CHAPTER TEN

Billy forced himself to eat a full, fried breakfast, even though it was now half-past two in the afternoon. Billy mulled the thoughts over in his head. The ability, this power that had somehow sprung as if from nowhere, was capable of tremendous acts, whether they be for good or evil (Perhaps, Billy thought that should be Good and Evil). Come to really think about it, who was to say what was good and what was evil? But regardless, Billy was scared. It wasn't just that he was painting, it was that he had no apparent control over it.

What if I do? What if I can control it? Billy wondered. Would it be wrong of him to paint himself with Laurel wrapped around him like a winter skin? Would he paint himself extravagantly wealthy? A millionaire, hell!, a billionaire! Would he paint himself successfully back in the ring competing? Would he paint world peace? Or would the power take over and make him paint things he didn't want to see when he thought he was still in control?

Laurel. Would he tell her? Ever? It was something he felt he wanted to share with her, but having said that, he wanted to share everything. All that he'd done in his life, all that Laurel had done in her life. Yes, it was true that she'd shared knowledge with Billy about their lives at dinner, but he was now thinking about talking, really talking. Which reminded him-

'Shit! I'm supposed to phone her!'

He rushed into his bedroom and took his mobile phone out of its charger on the bedside cabinet. He paused and looked at it for a silent second or two. Should he call her now? His mind was still racing about the paintings and he truly didn't trust himself not to blab about them over the phone, and he thought it best not to reveal something like the art work over the phone.

But what if she thought I wasn't bothering to call her? She might think I'm no-longer interested or just can't be bothered. Isn't that the game, though? If you call too soon she'll think you're over-eager, if you call too late she'll think you don't care. What to do? What...to...do?

Billy went for a run.

The beach was quiet, too peaceful for Billy's liking. His tired, burning thigh muscles pumped his legs and carried him forward through the loose sand. He had decided to run along dunes, the white sand stretching between himself and the ocean. Up and down the dunes, the sand giving way beneath him on his ay down, the loose covering sliding away as he attempted to gain purchase with his aching feet. He got to the peak of a dune hill, and stopped running. He arched his spine, pushing his hips forward, his head tilted back so he was looking skyward, even though his eyes were closed, his face a twisted grimace. His hands were on his hips, allowing his lungs to inflate to their fullest as he gulped in great swallows of air.

The sea was beautiful. It reflected the bright yellow-orange sun like a distorted mirror. The ocean looked cool and Billy could imagine the feeling of having the cold liquid rush down his throat, down his gullet and into his stomach, his chest growing icy. The stench of seaweed was carried up on the breeze and assaulted his sense of smell. He looked out to the sea, and his gaze focused on the horizon. Distant lands, distant worlds. He'd go off, far, far away over the horizon and leave the troubles of his life behind. Billy began to think that maybe, just maybe, he was over-reacting. What exactly is your biggest problem right now, Billy-boy?

Well, my biggest problem is that I'm not too sure when the best time to call an incredibly beautiful woman is.

Oh yeah, Billy-boy, big problem there.

Billy returned home, showered, and downed three large glasses of water before feeling comfortable enough to do anything else. Even then he had to discipline himself not to drink another glassful, for fear of making himself sick. He waited five minutes just to see if the water was going to play havoc with his guts, and then jotted down on a piece of paper a few conversational points. How are you? I really enjoyed last night. I'm well, thank you. Would you like to go out again?

He lifted the phone, his finger hovering over the keypad. He decided now was too soon to call her, so he put the phone back down. Then again, Billy thought, now might be the perfect time to call her. He raised the phone to his face again, and again put the phone down before having a chance to dial. 'Damn it man!' he scolded himself. He held the phone up, then put it down. Lifted. Placed it down. This continued for longer than Billy would have liked, although he had no concept of how much time had actually passed. It could have been a few seconds or it could have been several hours. In actuality it had taken roughly seven minutes.

'Hello you.'

Her voice was bubbly and friendly and happy once he'd finally summoned up the courage to call Laurel. He was, it's safe to say, pleasantly surprised. He had been expecting to catch her at a bad time, during the middle of some cheap daytime TV show or when she was in the shower or something.

'No, I was just pottering. So, what you been up to?'

'Just went for a run.' Of all the things she could have asked him that was the question he'd hoped she wouldn't. Billy knew Laurel would not want to hear, and would probably not believe him, if he started on about the paints.

'Oh, working up a sweat, were you?'

Billy was always disarmed by her flirtatiousness. He wasn't exposed to it too often and he didn't know how to deal with it when he was. Should he stay quiet only opening his mouth to release a school-girl-like giggle? Should he reply in kind and risk saying something wildly inappropriate? Should he ignore it and pretend he didn't pick up on it and risk her thinking he's a brain dead idiot? Or, should he worry so much about how to handle the situation that he ends up ignoring what she's saying to him right now?

Pay attention, dumb-ass!

'So what do you say?'

Oh come on! You've got to be kidding me! Not again? Well, what now, numb nuts?

'Sorry,' Billy began, 'the line's a bit dodgy at my end, what was that last thing?'

'I asked, "so what do you think?"'

'No, what do I say to what?'

'What? You've lost me.'

'Didn't realise I had you,' Billy whispered under his breath.

'Mmm, play your cards right,' Laurel whispered, sending a tingle through Billy's groin.

He could imagine her now, a broad, sexy smile plastered on her face as she lay belly-down on her bed, her ankles up in the air and crossed behind her, twirling the phone cord around her fingers. Billy caught himself wondering exactly where he got these types of images.

'So you in?'

Shit! Are you, are the fates taking the piss here? Once again, you've managed to miss what she's talking about, Billy-boy!

Deciding to take the most drastic action he was comfortable with, Billy spoke up.

'Would you like to go do something tonight?'

'You mean like bowling?'

'Uh, yeah, okay.'

'You haven't been listening to a word I've said, have you?'

'Um...yes?'

'You liar,' she was smiling and Billy could sense it.

'Is that what you were saying?'

'What do you think?'

'I'm sorry, my mind's been all over the place.'

'Don't worry about it. I'll pick you up in a little while.'

She hung up on him, and he was glad about it, slightly relieved. He really hated those couples who annoyed the hell out of their friends by constantly repeating, "No, you hang up. No, you hang up." Did those people not realise that they were in danger of being killed by the people around them, especially the single ones? My God, how annoying! Billy was looking forward to that stage with Laurel.

***

Bowling. Truly the sport of...of...of people who loved the competitiveness of sport without the pesky hassle of actual exertion. You had two clearly different groups at the bowling alley. At one end you had the young couples and rowdy teens on birthday trips. The people that stepped over the line at the start of the lane and nobody cared. The people who pretended to show their girlfriends correct technique purely as an excuse to hold them tightly in a vertical spoon.

Then you had the other group. The group that turned up wearing matching team shirts. The group that called every little infraction of the rules that were in the book, every possibility that this group might just have their own rule book (yes, they've written an actual, physical book) that has better defined rules. This was the group that brought their own shoes (and who could blame them, really?), the had their own balls with their names, or nicknames that were mostly self-attributed such as Lord of the Lanes and Marble Balls, engraved. This group wouldn't tolerate any physical contact between two people, maybe a celebratory high-five if they were playing in a team tournament (the rule book stated you could hold hands with your spouse, but why on Earth would you want to bring your spouse?).

Tally Bowl-A-Rama (why are they always called Bowl-A-Ramas?) was filled with the sound of low rumbling as balls travelled at considerable speed down the polished-to-reflection wooden floors of the lanes, intent on high-impact collisions with the pins. Occasionally the hollow explosion of pins being knocked down could be heard over the laughter from the young, and the sombre, grumpy grumbling of the old boys, all of whom wore wrist-supports and matching shirts. Often a strong smell of fast-food burgers and hot-dogs wafted over from the restaurant situated at the front of the building and took up most of the store-front window.

Billy was relieved to find Laurel didn't bring her own ball, although he could easily imagine her taking aim with a bright pink one with a large black L in script on it. He wondered how this would all go down, if it would be a couple of hours full of laughter or if it would be the last time they saw each other outside of what would become a very awkward art class. And, Billy-boy, don't even consider keeping score, you never keep score when playing a game with someone you, shall we say, like? You keep score when playing a game with your friends (just ask those guys over there with the huge bellies and matching shirts), but when you play with someone you want to…well, you play for the fun of it.

'Do you know how to keep score with these things?' she asked.

'No,' he answered honestly.

'Me neither,' she said pulling on an ugly red and blue bowling shoe. She knew at that moment that she must really, really like Billy a whole lot. That shoe was hideous. 'Sure we'll pick it up.'

'You bowled before, Laurel?' he made the effort to say her name at the end of his question. He'd read somewhere that saying the persons name was supposed to be good for this type of thing. It made the person feel comfortable and made them friendlier or something like that.

They tied the laces of the shoes, trying not to think of how many other pairs of feet, stinking, sweaty, fungus-infected feet, had been in them. They could see from where they were sat that when shoes were returned after a gruelling game, they weren't cleaned, just sprayed with some air-freshener.

'Do you want to go first?' she asked, suddenly very aware that neither of them had said anything for a short while. She was also very aware that the air-conditioner had brought her nipples up and she was quite happy for Billy to see them like that.

'You can, if you want.' Billy tried not to notice the peanuts Laurel was smuggling in her top. 'Not too sure I even know how to, if I'm honest.'

'Well don't look to me for advice, I'm less than useless.'

'I highly doubt that,' Billy smiled.

'I meant at bowling, she said standing up. 'But keep the compliments coming.'

(Not the only thing that will be coming)

Christ, Billy-boy, control your mind.

Laurel wiggled her way over to the balls racked up, and tested the weight of two, and then decided on the ball she was going to use. It was green, but darker than the green of her eyes. She slipped three of her slender digits into the grip holes, letting the pad of her finger tips caress the outer-edged of the holes first for Billy's benefit. She brought the ball up to her jaw, running her free hand over the smooth green surface. Billy couldn't be sure, but he thought he saw her lips moving in silent prayer to the ball, or the gods of bowling.

Well done, Billy-boy, I think we've just found out why she looks like that and yet is still single.

'Here I go,' she said smiling and raising her eyebrows. 'Wish me luck.'

Laurel stood at the end of the lane, took three carefully placed paces back, then brought her arm back and swung it forward and she moved the three paces forward. Just as she was about to release the ball, Billy yelled, 'Good luck.' the break in her concentration resulted in the ball rolling forward at an angle, and rocketing into the gutter.

She turned slowly to find Billy's mischievous face grinning back at her.

'Think we're funny, do we?'

'You told me to wish you luck.'

'I'm taking another go. And no cheek from you this time.'

Again, Laurel went through her three-paced ritual and prayer, and rolled the ball perfectly through the ten pins. The ball struck the very middle pin, sending them all tumbling, the explosion of wood-knocking wood as the pins collided with each other resonated throughout the alley.

'Stee-rike!' she called out.

Billy told himself not to mess his go up.

'Where are you going?' she asked as she stood waiting for her ball to be returned.

'Don't I get a go now?'

'Yeah, after me,' she told him hoisting the ball up.

It was at some point between Laurel lifting the ball and her second strike that Billy realised that maybe Laurel wasn't the novice she claimed to be.

'Stee-rike!'

It was Billy's turn. He swallowed hard and rose to his feet. Telling himself over and over again that he could do this, there was nothing to it, it was all well within his capabilities and then he realised he was giving himself a pre-fight pep-talk he gave himself, and countless others, before a boxing bout. He looked down at the balls for a few moments, picking up a ball or two and testing its weight, but not really know why. Other than weight, what exactly was a person supposed to look for in a ball?

'You okay there?' Laurel asked.

He didn't dare turn around to face her, for fear that his face would give him clear away. 'Yes,' he lied. 'I'm fine.' He wondered then briefly why it was that men, not mankind but just men, felt the need to do this? Why did they lie when just simply admitting there was a problem would probably bring about help much quicker? That voice in his head told Billy to hurry up, the beautiful woman had started to notice something was amiss.

Billy reached down and plucked the first ball his hand touched. It was covered in purple flames and had a fantasy art depiction of the Grim Reaper, his face a flesh-less skull with mad, soul-seducing eyes that glowed red on it. A crooked, black smile of sharp, jagged and pointed teeth was nestled under the psycho eyes. In its bony left hand it held a scythe, the index finger of its right hand was out-stretched and seemed to be pointing directly at Billy.

You, Billy. That black crooked smile whispered to him. I

know your secret, and I know what business is.

'Try this one,' Laurel said, suddenly standing at his side, holding a black ball.

'I know.'

'Of course you do.'

'I was just looking...admiring the art work.'

'I'll believe you,' she said. 'Thousands wouldn't.'

'I think I used to go out with her,' Billy said taking one last glance down at the Grim Reaper with the red eyes and crooked smile.

The ball was released from his grip much like Laurel had done, the three steps and everything, only when she let go of the ball it landed gently and rolled smoothly towards the pins. When Billy let go of the ball it first sailed through the air before bouncing with a series of thuds and thumps, eventually dropping into the gutter. It rolled down to the end of the lane, slipped behind the pins it never threatened and disappeared from sight.

'Smooth,' Laurel said sarcastically.

Thinking quickly Billy told her, 'I just did that so you wouldn't feel so bad about what you did on your first go.'

Ah yes, her first go. All those strikes ago.

'Really?' she quizzed. 'How thoughtful.'

'Do I get another go?'

'Do you hell.'

The second date was a bit different than the first. For starters Billy didn't recall getting absolutely hosed on the first date. As he'd instructed himself, Billy didn't keep track of the score. Originally that had been to maintain the playful air of two people just enjoying each others company. It had become because he couldn't bare to look at the numbers anymore; he was losing, and badly.

'You know,' Billy started, 'if at any point you feel like giving me any pointers here, feel free.'

'Well I was going to, only I didn't want you to feel emasculated.'

'Because nothing makes me feel all manly like losing?'

Laurel cocked her smiling head to the side as she shrugged before sitting down to take the ugly, horrendous bowling shoes off. The game was over, the end, home time, thank God. Billy leant over and proceeded to work loose the main knot on his laces.

'What are you doing?' Laurel asked, almost insulted.

'Taking my shoes off.'

'You've got a go left. Your turn to bowl.'

Billy stared at her beautiful, yet deadly serious face for a brief moment. Surely she's, no, no, she's not kidding. That crazy woman is actually expecting me to stand up and bowl one last frame, as if it would, or possibly even could, have any baring on the outcome of the game.

He stared at her eyes, then turned and looked down the lane to where the pins stood, mocking his inability to knock them over. 'You serious?' he asked.

'Absolutely.'

'Well here I go then.'

He didn't even bother to re-tie the off-white lace on his shoe, deciding to just tuck the loose ends into the side of the shoe. He didn't even bother about technique with this last one, he just hurled the black ball towards the pins with all of his might, wanting to get this ordeal over with as quickly as possible. The rumbling sound rolled to the distance and was followed quickly by the hollow breaking sound of pins falling over. 'Oh,' he remarked at his best roll yet.

'Yeah-yeah, whatever.' Laurel commented as she slipped two hooked fingers into the backs of those stomach-churning shoes.

The June air was still warm outside when they left the bowling alley (Bowl-A-Rama, for crying out loud!), and a more pleasant summer's evening Billy couldn't remember. Of course, had it been pouring with heavy rain and locust, Billy still would have thought it one of the best summer evenings he'd ever experienced. Laurel was the only thing he needed to have a good time.

'So what do you want to do now?' she asked as they made their way across parking lot. He looked her up and down like a piece of very sexy meat, and before he could say anything she added, 'Cheeky.'

Billy's face went bright red, bordering on pink, with embarrassment. He didn't realise she was looking at him, watching him, and if he did he certainly wouldn't have been so careless about eyeing her up. He didn't want to put across the impression that he was only interested in sex.

'No,' he defended. 'I didn't mean that.'

'Really?'

'Yeah. No,' he motioned up and down her body, 'it's nothing.

'And just what the hell does that mean?' she asked with mock-sternness. She laced her arm around his and clasped his hand with inter-lacing fingers. They continued walking, the warm breeze having a cooling effect on Laurel's chest, her nipples were so erect they were bordering on being painful, but she liked the attention they were getting from Billy's sly, side-glances.

'You should know that I don't really date a lot,' she told him.

Billy wondered why she was telling him this. She was talking now in much less jovial terms than before, no-longer was hers the voice of control. Her voice, for the first time since he'd met her, was full of uncertainty and insecurity. Gone was the strong, confident woman, here was the scared, timid weak young girl.

They continued walking around the parking lot without noticing that it wasn't the most romantic place in the world.

'I just want you to know that I haven't put myself about, or anything like that.'

Billy nearly choked on his laughter, 'I didn't think you had.'

'I just wanted to you to know that I'm sort of serious about this, about us...is that weird?'

'Why would it be weird?' he asked with a smile.

'Well, just because it's only our second date-'

'So?' he interrupted.

'So I don't want you to think I'm getting all clingy.'

'Honey,' he told her looking her in the eye, 'you feel free to cling to anything that comes to hand.'

'You know what I mean.'

And he did, he knew exactly what she meant, primarily because he felt the same. There was some resistance to out-right declaring any emotional attachment to one another, but at the same time if they never ever dated anyone else and spent the rest of their time together in this life they'd be perfectly happy.

They continued walking.

CHAPTER ELEVEN

Billy's sleep was restless and broken, sweat rose up out of every pour on his body. The covers were a rumpled pile on the floor, the sheet beneath him was un-tucked and creased under his writhing, thrashing body.

Images crossed his mind, floating past like paper boats sailed down a stream, slow and gentle. Images of destruction. Images of perfection. Images of forces he didn't know but strongly recognised. Images of places he knew intimately but had never been to. Some images were gone as soon as they arrived. Some images hung around like a bad smell, lingering like a racial slur.

He was vaguely aware of being awake, stumbling off the bed and kicking his leg free of the sheet that had wrapped itself around his ankle, clinging it to like a man-eating creature, an octopus with its many gripping and grappling limbs. He thought he could remember falling out of the doorway to his bedroom, the bruises dotted about his body would bring back memories of bouncing off walls and doorways. Still half-seduced by sleep, Billy ricocheted his way off the walls through the short hallway and into the room with the painting equipment in, and began to create, or discover, another depiction of terror.

A time or two, his muscled legs gave way beneath his weight, the weight of the situation, resulting in his slumping to the ground sending the pallet and the brush skidding across the floor and bumping into the walls and the foot of the door. The next morning there were tiny splashes of paint on the walls, no higher than two inches from the floor.

When he awoke later that morning, Billy had lost quite a bit of fluid from his body, and not just from sweat. As he'd fallen he'd smashed his face somehow, busting his lip and giving him a nasty cut on his eyebrow. His head hurt like a freight train had ploughed through it several times and he was certain that every cell in his brain was about to die. He could feel his brain drying out and withering like an un-watered plant at the height of a summer heat wave.

Another concern was his shorts. They were stuck to his legs and hips as though someone had poured a fine glue over the top of them. In parts the dampness had dried a little, leaving a glittering crusty stain in its wake. Billy knew what it was, and seriously began to wonder why this was happening. The rest of it, the fore-telling of gratuitous events, didn't even enter the equation anymore, he just wanted to know about the sex drive. Always when he painted, he felt an incredible urge to get laid. His thoughts turned to Laurel-

(Brave in the circumstances)

and worried what would happen in the next art class if he suddenly erupted mid-stroke (of his paint brush). He couldn't see even Laurel being okay with that type of behaviour. As he moved, the shorts clung to him like a sticky second skin. He was reminded of putting on wet clothes, the way the cloth slapped onto your skin and clung there.

He felt dizzy as he rose, seeing everything in the small room in triplicate and revolving around, all edges fuzzy and hazy. He put an arm out and leant against the wall for stability, rubbing his eyes. When he opened his eyes again, there was now only one of everything and although he was experiencing dancing black dots in front of him for a few seconds. When his vision cleared and returned to 20/20, he cast his gaze over to the easel, his body shaking slightly form anticipation of what he might see painted on the top page staring back at him.

'What the...?' his voice trailed off to a croak before stopping.

He saw, but he didn't understand.

A beautiful green field, no, this wasn't a mere field, it was a meadow, a spring meadow! A crystal-blue river ran across the bottom of the page, the very southern-most point of the green meadow. A bright, loving, yellow-orange sun was rising in the clear, soft- blue sky above. The picture seemed to radiate a warmth, Billy was scared that the picture was actually glowing. Three people stood in the centre of the meadow, their faces unmarked by features, but clearly identifiable from their clothes. One wore a long white robe, one wore a bright gold shirt and matching hat, and the other a t-shirt and blue trousers. All stood in a line, holding hands.

Billy knew what it meant. He knew what it would mean for future generations. It meant peace. It meant actual world peace.

World Peace.

Imagine the possibilities. No more war. No more need for weapons. All that money, trillions and trillions each year, no longer spent on ways to kill each other, but used on feeding the hungry, clothing the naked, educating the ignorant, not one single person left out or neglected. All those many more people being put through school means more people going off and becoming doctors and nurses and scientists and increasing the chances of one of our children discovering the cure for cancer, the Big C, or AID's. Who knows what else? A world where everyone gets a fair shake. Regardless of what colour your skin is. Regardless of what gender you are. Regardless of what deity you kneel before. No more racism, no more sexism, no more homophobia, no more teens being beaten because they listen to music made by men who wear make-up.

Think of the break-through's. Think of how much more we could discover, all as one, together, no more hate, no more fear. Just love, pure, unadulterated love. Imagine it. No more intolerance. Every single human being hating their neighbour because their neighbour plays music too loud or because their neighbour's an jackass. But not because of their nationality, or their gender or religion.

A world of peace.

No more parents crying as a man who was in the same company tells them their son stood on an anti-tank mine. No more pregnant wife pacing at home worried that her baby's father might not be coming home from a war in the desert. No more proud father holding back tears looking at pictures of his daughter when she was three and in her ballet tutu, hoping that she made the right choice when she enlisted. No more war casualties, as there'd be no more war.

World Peace.

And the truly frightening thing, the really, honestly scary part is that eve of world peace didn't lie within the reach of a world leader. No politician could flick a switch or take the vote to bring it about. But the most horrifying thing was the power lay with an artist. A simple, pure artist, could bring it about. If only he knew how to harness the power he was just now discovering he had.

CHAPTER TWELVE

Two more weeks went by, bringing with them two more art classes, and several more dates, although in all honesty they didn't really tick all the boxes to qualify as dates. It was usually just the bare essential. Him. Her. Her laughter. Good times. Enjoyment. They were having a picnic on a stretch of closely-cropped grass, basking and relaxing in the early afternoon sun, when the relationship talk really began. Billy, bless him, was content enough just being with her. The headaches very rarely came now, and he really couldn't remember if he'd ever had that sledge-hammer pounding away in his head when he was around Laurel (he was sure, however, that he always had that ticking time bomb in his underwear constantly when he was around her).

'So, what do you think?' she asked him with large, expectant eyes.

'I think you're beautiful.'

'That's not what I asked.'

'Okay, I think you're pretty smart, too.'

'Sometimes,' she propped herself up on her elbows and leant towards him, 'you're a creep.'

'I'm always a creep,' he said leaning in to her, 'just most times I'm decent enough to try to hide it.' He concluded with a light peck on her cherry red lips.

'I meant, what do you want to do about tonight?'

'I'm happy doing whatever you want to do.'

'Are you now?' she asked with a cheeky smile.

'Yeah, why?'

'You really don't listen to me when I talk, do you?'

'I try,' he said, 'it's just I'm so mesmerised by your-'

'Yeah-yeah,' she interrupted. 'I'm gorgeous, you can't believe you're with me, heard it all before.'

'Fine then,' he mock-sulked. 'Won't bother next time.'

She released a sigh and glared at him. He was hard work at times, but it was a good type of hard work. He made her crazy. And not just the, ooh I'm so crazy about him kind of crazy, but the if you don't shut up I'm squashing your balls in a vice type of crazy. But, even so, there was something about him, something there that told her he was all good, or mostly good with just the right amount of bad to make things interesting.

'I asked if you wanted to stay over at my place tonight.'

'You mean...like...' his head bobbed about on the end of his neck. How men had assumed that motion to mean sex, Laurel didn't know, would never know, and only hoped that it wasn't something that they thought a girl might like in the bedroom. She tensed her face in a hopeful, half-closed smile, and nodded with sharp, sudden jolts of her head.

'As in...staying over?' he continued.

More sudden nodding.

'Until the morning?' he edged closer to her.

She nodded slowly, the smile nothing more than a sexy pout now, her left eyebrow raised.

'Together?' he kissed her before she could answer him, and they fell back into the red, plaid blanket that laid beneath them in the park, locked in a mutual embrace.

'Be at my place by seven,' she told him once he finally came up for air and freed her mouth. She felt a strong tingle, a surge, rush to her groin and it grew warm and bothersome. It was a feeling of pure desire and it was making a nuisance of itself.

'I will,' he said as he brushed a stray strand of hair from her forehead.

'Good. And not a minute before, I've got to get rid of my other boyfriends first.'

'Ha-ha,' he said dryly. 'That's not funny, you know?'

'I'll take your word on what's not funny.'

'I can be funny.'

'Funny looking.'

'Pot, kettle, black.'

'Hey, do you want to come 'round tonight or not?'

'I'll be good.'

'Shame. I'll be very, very naughty,' she said licking her lips, her voice hushing down to a sexy whisper. Laurel caught sight out of the corner of her eye of what she'd affectionately come to think of as Billy's Bulge and she couldn't wait for seven o'clock.

Billy's face showed anxiety, anticipation and excitement all at once, though Laurel had to stifle a laugh as the thought popped into her mind that Billy looked like he might have gas. The best way to stifle a laugh? Chew someone face off. She leaned forward, draped her left arm over the back of his neck, and pulled him on top of her.

CHAPTER THIRTEEN

Laurel's apartment was exactly what Billy had expected it to be; small, with basic, yet sensible, colour schemes. The living room was dominated by a large, soft, red couch, with large cushions that just gobbled you up when you sat on, and then sunk into, them. The apartment was on the fifth floor, and had a decent enough view of the city and an unbeatable view of the park. She could easily pick out the spot she'd been lying on with Billy earlier in the day.

The scent of thick, Italian sauce filled the rooms as it wafted from the small kitchen where Laurel was hard at work preparing that evening's meal. It was going to be pasta in a red sauce, with wine. Lots of wine. Not too much though, wouldn't want anyone to be unable to perform (Laurel had forgotten that Billy didn't drink).

Billy entered through the opened front door that was just pushed to (Laurel had opened it after Billy had buzzed up via the intercom. He did not think he would tell her that he got the apartment number wrong the first time and had spent several minutes apologising profusely to Mr and Mrs Chang who also lived in the building), and called in to the apartment.

'I'm in here,' Laurel called back to Billy as he closed the front door. He passed along the hallway and entered the kitchen, which looked like a fall-out zone. A large steel pot was simmering on the hob, many dancing twists of pasta scrunched together under the bubbling water, steam slowly rising up from it. Billy wondered if by the end of the night he and Laurel would be pressed up that tightly together. He stood behind her and wrapped his arms like creeping boa constrictors around her taut waist and held her closely to him, breathing her scent in. His slightly engorged penis pushing down against her firm, curved buttocks.

'Easy,' she told him. 'Plenty of time for that later.'

'How long 'til it's ready?'

'I'd guess it's ready right now.'

'I meant the food.'

'Oh,' she turned around in his arms to face him, pushing her body close against him. 'That'll be about twenty minutes,' she said before kissing him passionately.

'Twenty minutes is more than enough time,' he joked.

'No.'

'Really, it is. Ten minutes, tops. Five if I think of my tutor in college.'

'Hey!' she slapped his arm playfully.

'Three minutes if we cut out the foreplay. Ninety seconds if you talk dirty.'

'You're not helping your case here, y'know?'

They kissed again, and a short while later, after they'd eaten and Laurel had consumed just the right amount of wine, she led Billy by the...hand into her bedroom. The bedroom was decorated in light and dark purples, including a huge, thick duvet spread over the king-size bed. Billy was hoping that duvet wouldn't be the only thing spread over that bed before sunrise.

She unbuttoned his shirt and took it off his shoulders as she allowed her hands to glide over his shoulders and chest, then down his torso, over his tight, hard abs. She kissed his strong pec muscles as her hands loosed his belt, before dropping to her knees in front of him and pulling down his trousers, bringing her eye-level with the long, thick bulge in his tight, form-hugging boxer shorts.

'Oh my!' she exclaimed.

'Huh?'

'Ssh.'

Billy nodded. Billy would have agreed with anything right now. It was so much better than any fantasy he'd had. She hadn't even began to touch him properly yet, and this was so, so, much better than any fantasy.

Laurel continued to kiss and caress his stomach as her hand gripped and stroked at Billy's throbbing penis beneath the grey cotton of his underwear. She stood up, kissed him deeply, and sat back on the bed, extending her long, slender and sexy left leg, rubbing the foot against Billy's erection. He held her foot gently but firmly and, whilst rubbing her foot with his hands, began to kiss down her calf. Bringing just the tips of his fingers down the lower half of her leg, his right hand stopping and massaging the spot at the back of her knee (which sent off mini fireworks in her brain, and began the tides of pleasure that washed through her body), as the fingers of his left hand slowly made their way down the inside of her thigh.

Billy began to shower small but firm and loving kisses down her thigh, then kissing the gusset of her French panties, before moving across and kissing down her right thigh, running his fingers along her hamstrings, strengthening the waves of pleasure she felt. Time and again, Billy kissed up and down the insides of both thighs, across the concealed opening of her increasingly wet vagina. He got onto the bed and kissed his way up her body until her powerful legs were wrapped around his hips, and began to kiss the left side of her neck. He kissed her mouth before brushing the hair away from her face, and looked deeply into her eyes.

'Laurel,' he said, 'I just want you to know before we do this, that I really like you.'

She nodded her head quickly and approvingly.

'I just don't want you to think that I'm-'

'Billy,' she interrupted. 'Don't take this the wrong way, but fucking get on with it.'

Billy leant down and kissed her deeply and lovingly. And lustfully. The kiss went on for a long time, all the while Billy couldn't stop thinking how unbelievably lucky he was. Laurel briefly thought the same, and then wished Billy would get back to the good stuff.

Possibly reading her very thoughts, Billy broke the kiss and made his way down her body. Once he reached her waist, she sat up quickly and reached behind her back to pull the zip down, allowing Billy to pull it off, revealing her tight, taut, toned body in nothing but skimpy black French panties and a strapless black bra. He stood up and looked down at her on the bed, her blond hair spread out beneath her head like sunbeams.

'You just going to stand there salivating?' she asked tracing a foot along the inside of his thigh and up to his powerful package. 'Or are you going to get to work?'

He knelt down and pulled Laurel's panties off, then traced the opening of her very wet vagina with his tongue, as his fingers played over her stomach in circles, and then moved up her body and under her bra to play with her firm breasts. Her body convulsed and gyrated with each twirl of his tongue. He removed his boxers and got onto the bed.

'Wait, wait,' she whispered breathlessly, bringing a momentary halt to proceedings. she reached over the side of the bed and brought up a wooden box that hard a swirling pattern carved on the top. Billy thought it looked like the past they'd had earlier. Laurel lifted the lid on its tiny, clover-leaf shaped hinges and threw a small blue foil square at Billy, who, naturally had trouble getting the condom out of its packaging.

'Should I ask how many of these you've got in there?'

'Don't worry,' she purred as she sat, stroking and kissing his stomach. 'I don't expect us to go through them all tonight.'

'I am glad.'

'We've tomorrow morning as well.'

Billy rolled the light blue condom onto his hard, pulsating penis, laid down on top of Laurel, got comfortable, and penetrated her. She drew a sharp breath, and then smiled uncontrollably as Billy began to move in her.

They brought each other to a simultaneous climax.

They made love three more times that night before finally coming to a rest.

Laurel fell asleep with Billy's left arm around her, her left arm across his chest, still glistening from a light sheen of sweat Billy kissed her forehead and then himself drifted into sleep.

***

His thoughts were hazy, his arms, shoulders and the back of his neck felt old, almost to the point that the bones beneath the skin began to ache. The bottom two feet of his body was lost to a low, creeping white fog, Stuff ghosts are made of, Billy thought.

A hallway. Billy told himself that he was in a hallway, but he didn't know where. Or why. He wondered almost absently about where Laurel was. The hallway was strangely familiar to him, but still strangely disorientating. It wasn't Laurel's place, but his own. He asked himself if he'd come back here after being with Laurel, but didn't think that was right. He was head-over-heels happy to be there with her, so why would he leave? He wasn't the type of man to run out on a girl after sex, and especially not after what he'd done with-to!-Laurel and he didn't think he'd want to leave after that.

Billy put his arms out to his sides trying to place his hands on the walls to steady himself, only the walls were not so close to hand. He turned to his left to see the all-black wall slowly creep away from him. His mind raced, he sucked his teeth pulling his lips back over the gums, making a 'tssk' sound. Had he ever done that before? No, no it was Billy's father that used to do that. He always did that. Usually when he was reeking of cheap whiskey and just about to beat the tar out of someone. More often than not Billy or his mother.

He moved forward along the hallway, afraid that the floor beneath his feet and hidden by the ghostly fog could, and would, at any moment turn into thick, goopy marshland, deep and black with long-reaching green weeds, that stretched out like thick but strong fingers pulling you down deep. One misplaced foot step and Billy could see himself drowning in black water and mud. Rather than lifting his feet, he was barely gliding them over the ground, removing the chance of tripping over something.

A door suddenly appeared to his right, bright white to the point that it caused slight pain to actually look at it head-on. It slowly crept open slightly by itself, more of that eerie ghostly white fog wove its way out of the gap.

Forcing himself to go on as the fear bubbled up in his belly, Billy entered the room. The sudden drop in temperature bringing his skin up in goose-bumps. It was only now that he saw he was naked except for the grey boxer shorts that were now as tight as skin, easily two-sizes too small. At first he could make nothing in the room out, his eyes hurting with the glare, the glow, everything in the room was giving off. Before his vision came to him, he could smell it. That same thick, putrid, chemical smell.

The smell of paint.

'No-no-no!' Billy raged to himself in the room, rubbing his temples. 'Not again, no more. No more.'

Only, that wasn't quite true. He wasn't alone in the room. He couldn't see anyone else, he couldn't hear any movement, but he could sense, in a very real way, someone, or something, else in there with him. He slowly opened his eyes, and waited for them to adjust to the light, only that blinding glow was gone. The room was lit in a frosty, blue light. Sat on a table, with his feet on the floor, at the far end of a room was a Japanese man, wearing a long black robe that was very baggy at the sleeves, and lined with a blue trim. He had, Billy thought, black hair that was combed back, and a black moustache. In this light at this distance, Billy couldn't be sure of anything he saw.

'Who are you?' Billy asked, confused and scared.

'Who is of no importance. Only why.'

Billy waited, then asked, with some annoyance, 'Okay, then why am I here?'

'To see me.'

'Why are you here then?' Billy asked, already any and all patience he may have had for these games was gone.

'To tell you. To help you see.'

'See what?'

'I'm getting to that.'

Billy took a deep breath to calm himself, but as he inhaled he felt the sharp stabbing pain of the boxer's waistband digging into him. The Japanese man remained where he was and stayed perfectly still, only his mouth moved. It was only then that Billy realised just how much people gesticulated when they spoke.

'You have discovered a tremendous power, Mr Heath,' the Japanese man said in perfect English. 'You no doubt are already aware.'

'Yes,' Billy said, barley.

'The images that you discover, they sometimes bring about bad things. More often than not though, they bring about good.'

This stopped Billy, not that he had bee moving, really. He thought about everything he'd drawn, sketched, painted, created. No, not created, discovered. surely Denis's wife being hit can't be considered a good thing-

'No, of course not,' the Japanese man said. He was reading Billy's mind. 'No, not your mind. Just your thoughts.'

Was there a difference? Billy couldn't tell, right now, it was hard to work out.

'You are like a small child with a machine gun, Mr Heath. In the right hands it is a very useful thing, in the wrong hands, hands such as yours, or a child's, it brings un-told horrors.'

'I don't know what you're getting at.'

'Of course not. Consider this; most of the things you've painted brought about good, correct?'

Nodding, Billy knew it wasn't really a question. He also got the feeling that the man in the darkness could really put a hurting on him, should the mood take him.

'Good, then we're in agreement. You have recently un-locked powers that you did not know you had. We did not know you had them, either. Had we done, we would have found you a lot sooner.'

Who the we in question were, Billy had no idea, at this time he didn't think it was overly important. He did, however, have a strong feeling that this would not be the time to zone out as he had done many times with Laurel.

'If you focus, and train your mind and body and stop let-ting...urges, control you, then you could have unknown power at your disposal.'

Billy sensed that the Japanese man who spoke perfect Eng-lish was not searching for the word urges but rather found the word distasteful. It somehow cheapened him just saying it.

'You have been suffering sever side-effects from your cre-ativity.'

'Yes. Headaches. Sometimes I get a nose bleed, nothing major.'

'No, I mean your brain stops working because you get the need for fuckie-fuckie.'

This brought a smile to Billy's face. Up to that point he had been equal parts in awe and fear of the mysterious man in the robe, but now he sounded like a stereotypically racial cartoon character.

'Good, I'm glad that made you smile. Only a very few are born with the gift, Mr Heath. Most never find the catalyst to start it. Very few who do find their Muse to fuel it. Do you understand?'

Nodding and smiling, Billy honestly answered, 'Not a fuck-ing clue.'

'Very well. You have the power to bring about what every-one always dreams of-'

'World peace?'

'Yes. But please, Mr Heath, this will work better if you don't interrupt me-'

'I'm sorry.'

The Japanese man's face frowned, at least Billy thought it did. 'Your Muse, she is a powerful woman in her own right. You are fuelled by her, rather, your desire to be with her. Art is creative, it is joyous. It gives a man a sense of accomplishment. As does sex. What is more fulfilling to a man's creativity than creating life? Nothing. Your power is manifesting itself, but you are weak, Mr Heath.'

'Am I now?'

'Yes.' There was not a single sense of irony or anger in his voice. 'If you were able to control yourself, you would direct all of you power into the art, thereby controlling whether it was for good or bad.'

'Are yo saying that if I lay off the sex and paint, I can control what I paint?'

'In a way, Mr Heath, yes. you have recently cemented your relationship with the Muse. This will now strengthen your power. If you do not control this gift, Mr Heath, the bubble in your head will only get worse.'

Bubble? What bubble?

The Japanese man again read Billy's thoughts, and proceeded to explain. 'Your nose bleeds, Mr Heath. They are being caused by a tumour growing in your brain. When you get the desires that so distract you from your work, you throw away that power if you are alone. You had that desire, but you gave that power to your Muse, who in turn has unknowingly sent it back to you. That is what has allowed you to reach this plane, where we can meet at last.'

Billy thought about the man's words. Meet at last. Just how long has this guy been watching me? What, exactly, has this guy watched me doing?

'Please, Mr Heath, do not be embarrassed. It is purely a natural function of the body. Only, you must refrain until your work is completed.'

'No sex? We've only just-'

'No, Mr Heath. Sex is perfectly fine, encouraged, in fact. It gives you the strength. You must always give the power to your Muse, who in turn will return it to you. After your work is completed, you can do as you wish.'

'What work are you talking about?'

'The big work. The work you were born to do. The work that you must be sure to complete. The work you must give yourself to, entirely, until it is finished. You must finalise the art you began last.'

Billy's mind raced, he searched his memory quickly for the most recent work he had began. Then it hit him. Three men in a meadow. One wearing a white robe, one in a gold shirt with matching hat, one wearing a t-shirt and jeans. The crazy Japanese man was expecting Billy to bring about world peace, actual world peace, by splashing a few paints onto a canvas.

'What if I can't?' Billy asked at last.

The Japanese man appeared to bow his head, contemplating the best way to put in to words the awfulness of what would be if Billy could not finish his work. Finally, the Japanese man looked up and held eye contact with Billy, and then pointed to a space behind the young man. Billy turned around and wished he hadn't.

Laurel. Naked. Crucified on an easel. Her right leg was inverted, right knee crossed over the left, her head slumped and cocked to the left. A semi-circle of red paint ran down from across her collar bone and dribbled down her naked body, illuminated with a pale glow coming from...somewhere. Upon her head was a wreath made out of the small, red-brown paint brushes, all with their handles facing inwards, piercing the delicate soft skin of her brow.

Billy was transfixed. The best thing to happen to him in a long, long time was being executed in the most world-renown way on a symbol of an unearthly, horrifying power he had recently acquired. He was captivated by her still-open, lifeless eyes staring out vacantly at him. The tips of her blond hair were tinted red as they absorbed the blood. Her eyes were accusing him, he had done this. She was displayed in naked sin on the same canvas that he'd drawn up the blue-prints for terrible, terrible acts. How could you do this to me? She was asking in her silence. Billy stood, mouth agape, cheeks and forehead pal like the wax on a candle.

He tried to tell her he was sorry, he tried to explain that he didn't know what was going on here, that he wasn't responsible, that it wasn't his fault. He attempted to convey that he would never, there could never, be any motivation in the world, no reasoning ever in existence to prompt him to ever cause her any harm. He willed his body, his mouth, his vocal cords all he could, but still no sound came out. As much as he tried, he could emit no noise.

Her dead eyes and emotionless face echoed the sentiment in Billy's head; You have killed me you have killed me you have killed me.

No. I haven't. Really, I haven't.

You have killed me you have killed me you have-

No! I never would have. I can change it! Please, just give me some time! Please just let me change it, just give me the chance to paint over-

Paint!

Without any words being exchanged, between either Billy or the dead Laurel or Billy and the Japanese man, the message, albeit obvious, what Billy was looking at wasn't a painting, wasn't just another sketch, wasn't just another artistic interpretation. It was an actual person, a fully-grown human-being, crucified, stuck on the easel in front of him.

You

(no)

Have

(no)

Killed

(no)

Me

(NO!)

Billy stood up straight, rocked forward with a jerk, staring at a purple bedroom wall. A pale blue light crept in through the crack in the curtain, giving the room a faint tomb's glow.

'What?'

Laurel's voice called from the bed behind him. He could feel a warm, thin liquid had formed on his upper-lip. He brought the back of his hand up to his face and wiped his mouth, hesitating a brief moment before finally summoning the courage and forcing himself to look. He was relieved to discover it was sweat, not claret form the nose bleed he'd feared under his lip. He was standing naked at the far end of the bedroom, having got out of the warm, womb-like bed and sleepwalked over to where he was now. He noted a slight draught on his ankles from under the door and took that to be where his mind had created the ghostly fog.

'Are you okay, hon?' she asked as he turned around to face the bed. He nodded in darkened silence momentarily before realising she no doubt wouldn't be able to see his gesture.

'Yeah, I'm okay.'

'You gonna come back to bed?' she asked playfully. 'I would come over to you but I seem to have lost the use of my legs.'

He smiled slightly and could feel himself start to blush at the compliment to his sexual prowess. Had any girl ever been so forthright about anything bedroom related before? The first girlfriend he'd had that he slept with was far and away more experienced than he was and had a more Get On With It attitude. His second serious girlfriend really didn't think these types of things should be discussed, and she didn't even believe in Being Intimate with each other outside of the bedroom. There was something strangely arousing about having a very polite woman talking about your genitals and repeatedly using the word "cock."

Laurel broke out in a slight giggle that she was unable to stifle as Billy made his way back to the bed.

'What?' he questioned somewhat insecurely.

'Nothing.'

'No, go on. What is it?'

'It's just that when you walk...your cock swings back and forth like a pendulum.'

Oh. Well, that was perfectly acceptable for her to say, perhaps even something to be encouraged.

'So,' she said snuggling up to him as he climbed into the bed. 'You ready to go again?'

'Might be,' he replied with a cheeky grin before kissing her.

Her hand moved down his body and squeezed his growing penis, 'I'd say you're ready.'

CHAPTER FOURTEEN

Morning came shortly after Billy had succumbed to sleep after making love to Laurel, the fear of another dark, demonic dream coming to assault his psyche had kept the warm grip of slumber at bay for quite some time. Billy thought, if only fleetingly, that this was not the way forward, to constantly be afraid of falling asleep. It was a battle the human body just wasn't designed to win. You could stave off sleep through many different avenues; caffeine, pills, chemicals, but it's a war you can't win. Eventually, at some point, the body collapses, and sleep take you effortlessly.

Sleep can wait for you, because it knows it will win.

Laurel nudged Billy gently, which quite to her surprise snapped him awake instantly. His eyes opened wide before returning quickly to a squint as the harshness of the morning light attacked his pupils, a small, short groan rumbled up from his throat, and he rolled over, burrowing his face into her shoulder, turning his back to the window. She stroked the side of his face and pushed the hair back from his temples, her face in pout as she told him it was morning, and that it was time to get up.

'C'mon,' she joked,' time to get up.'

'That takes me back to last night.'

'Shut up, cheeky,' she slapped him playfully on the shoulder, 'and get dressed.'

She swung her sexy legs out from under the duvet and walked naked over to her wardrobe. It was a rare thing indeed to find a woman this comfortable and confident with her own body. She lifted up a very short silk robe that was draped over a rail (not hung up) and put it on, her breasts swaying. Billy thought if she'd always had such erotic movements or if it was all for show, all for him.

***

They entered Billy's small apartment with two completely different emotional states bubbling up under the surface. Laurel was a mix-bag of excitement and nervousness. She did have a vision of what Billy's place would look like. All black leather furniture and stainless steel framed tables and TV cabinets. A large framed picture on the wall of Muhammad Ali knocking out Sonny Liston (she'd done some research on boxing since meeting Billy). There would be a state-of-the-art stereo system, a TV so big it borders on being obtrusive, and a collection of DVD's so big it would elicit the 'you could start your own store' lame joke.

There would undoubtedly be a stack of what they called

"men's literature" probably by the side of the black leather sofa, and more than likely one or two serious films that were best-known for their gratuitous sex scenes. A collection of films by a particular actress wouldn't come as much of a surprise, though she didn't know if she'd refer the actress in question to bare a striking resemblance to her or look nothing like her at all.

It would be a typical bachelor pad, complete with every-thing a stylish man in his mid twenties would need to seduce a string of good-looking women.

What Laurel found was a living room with a battered old wooden book case that was overflowing with books, biographies and autobiographies and encyclopaedias of boxers and boxing. It seemed Billy was just as concerned with the life-story and how to heal people once you've broken them up. She thought that Billy could break her up anytime, and had a small fit of the internal giggles. The couch was not the black leather of the smooth oper-ator she had expected, but rather a red fabric one with a blanket thrown over the back and a small selection of comfortable cush-ions.

No man-orientated books or magazines, or at least none that she could see, but she thought that maybe they could be hid-den in a drawer or at the bottom of a wardrobe or some place. Not that she at all minded his having an eye for scantly-clad twits that couldn't count up to twenty-two without getting their tits out.

Although the apartment was tidy with books in their place and a few DVD's where they should be, but there was still a sense in the place that there were still things that he hadn't unpacked, as though Billy had only taken out the bare essentials.

'You wanna see me room?' Billy asked, wrapping his arms around Laurel's waist.

'Now why would I want to see your room?'

'Why not? Might see something you like.'

'See it? I can feel it.'

She placed her arms around his neck. She started to nuzzle the side of his neck, when she saw the white door. 'What's in there then?' she asked. Her focus was on the door, and no amount of groping or squeezing Laurel's firm body was going to get her back in the mood. Not even when Billy dragged his hand carefully along the crotch of her jeans, did she respond.

'What are you-oh.' Billy said turning to look in the same direction as Laurel. 'That, uh, that's just a room I keep my....my paint stuff in.'

'Your paint stuff?' Laurel asked, suddenly very interested.

'Yes. Why?'

'Have you got other paintings in there?

Before Billy had a chance to dissuade her, Laurel had slipped free of the sex-fuelled embrace, and was heading for the door. There was no worry. As she got close to the door, Laurel was struck by a sudden feeling of danger, real danger, in that room. Whatever was behind that door was awful , like a savage and hungry beast with blood lust.

Laurel thought she was picking up a negative vibe that, that couldn't be, could it? Was the room behind the door actually pulsating with violence and hatred and anger? Laurel could feel some...energy coming from behind that door, burrowing its way into her body. She felt sick, as though she'd been hungry for hours and then guzzled down pints of water rapidly. Her knees were very close to buckling, and it took all her strength not to turn tail and run.

She was reminded of years and years ago when she was only a little girl and the man three doors down from her grandmother had a Doberman that was always kept in the front yard. The only thing keeping that snarling beast from getting out and eating huge chunks out of everyone and anyone was a black steel gate that could barely hold the dog back. It's head was almost able to squeeze out between the bars of the gate and slip out to roam loose on the streets, tearing into humans like it did its toys.

Laurel had always hated walking past that gate, knowing that at any minute on the way past the ferocious, salivating head would lurch out from that gate and attempt to chomp at her. That was the feeling Laurel had now. Something was barely being held back, and it was ready at any moment to pounce out and bite through her neck.

'Are you sure you want to see them?

Billy's question broke her train of thought and brought her back to the here and now. No. The answer to his question, the answer Laurel wanted to give, was no. she in no way, shape or form wanted to go into that room for any reason, because whatever was in there certainly didn't want to see her. But she also knew deep down in that adult part of the brain that silences childhood instincts, that she had to go forward, she had to see what was behind that door.

Nodding, although not too sure why, she replied 'Yes. I'd like to see.'

Putting his arm around her shoulders, Billy led her forward as he pushed her forward as he pushed the handle down and opened the door, which swung into the room ominously. Come in, it whispered to her. If you dare. She had to go forth into the room and see whatever it was that was causing such irrational fear-terror!- in her.

A strong smell of paint that assaulted Laurel's sense of smell and made her eyes sting just a little filled the room, as she entered ahead of Billy, at his insistence. The walls were plain and had many pictures leaning on them. There they were, lined up against the walls, and gathered in stocks, and filled everywhere and anywhere. Hundreds of painted images depicting things that no mind should ever be able to conjure up. At random, Laurel picked up a painting and turned it around to look at the picture on the other side. She felt a million butterflies in her stomach.

'Oh...wow.' Laurel was suitably impressed as she saw a boxer with a title belt around his waist and bags of money. She was at first taken back by how realistic it looked. After searching some time for the words, not the right words, just any words, Laurel asked, 'Are they all like this?'

'No,' he answered. 'They're not all, well some are like, what do you mean?'

'This is really good,' she said honestly. 'You're really talented. Really. It's breath-taking.'

'I wish you'd said that last night,' he joked.

'Not everything revolves around that, you know?'

Laurel put the painting back where she picked it up from, and then lifted another up. She was already turning it around in her hands before Billy recognised what the painting was and could stop her. She was looking down at the picture that Billy had masterfully painted. What Laurel saw was herself in a tight blue dress.

'Oh Billy.'

'I can explain-'

'It's perfect.'

Billy was sunned, he was expecting Laurel to be annoyed. Maybe not so pleased that the man she was sleeping with had been painting portraits of her for quite some time. If you're married and you paint portraits of your wife, then that's romantic and sweet. If you're not even seeing each other socially, then painting a person time after time is really kind of creepy. He was expecting her to be completely freaked out at the thought of the man painting her so often and then sleeping with her.

Why would she be angry? Why wouldn't she be angry? She's a woman, they're all crazy, remember?

'You...you're not angry?' he asked.

'Why would I be angry?' she asked, not too sure why Billy

would expect her to be angry. 'You haven't got any of me nude, have you?'

'No,' he defended with a slight raise in his voice that he desperately hoped she didn't hear. Not so much that a rising pitch in his voice was a signal of guilt, it was just damned unmanly.

'I just thought it might look a little...I don't know, stalker-ish.'

'Is that even a real word?'

'Not really my point.'

'Well, you can stalk me anytime,' She said attempting that naughty, kinky smile she'd been flashing him since the first moment they kissed, but now it was fake, plastic, phony. She wasn't too sure if she wanted Billy anywhere near her at all, as it happened. But why? Why the sudden change of heart? Just a few short hours ago, she'd let him, willed him even, to be doing things to her that defied the laws of physics and the human body. Now she was sure she could feel her skin crawl. When Billy wrapped his arms around her shoulders, she jerked, jumping slightly.

She hoped that Billy, if he noticed at all, would just put her startled movement to being startled. She knew it was down to no-longer seeking his physical touch.

'I'm so glad you're not upset,' he whispered into her ear, a strong smell of coconuts clung to her hair. He kissed her cheek and nuzzled her ear, adding, 'I'd hate to lose you.'

Of course he would, she knew that. He wasn't lying, it wasn't a put-on. Laurel had been screwed over by enough pricks in her life to be able to tell when she was being lied to by a man. Right now, she was being told nothing but the honest truth by the man who had wrapped himself around her like a winter skin, and more than that, she felt safer, her stomach no-longer wanted to empty itself.

It wasn't Billy that was making Laurel feel ill. It was the room.

'So,' she said breaking loose from his grip and putting the portrait of herself back on the floor, 'want to show me the rest of your place?'

Even as the words left her mouth, Laurel knew deep down her motivation wasn't too see the rest of the apartment, she just wanted out of the room. Out of the room that had caused her to feel sick, made her feel extremely uncomfortable. It was the room, or something in it, that made her feel like screaming when she was touched by the man whom she'd spent all that time with.

Billy led Laurel out of the paint room and had walked half-way across the living room before returning to the room to close the door. A wave of relief washed over her at that point, a state of almost euphoric proportions came upon her. The further away she got from the contents of that room the better she felt. Against he own intelligent thoughts, she was sure that there really was something in that little room. A dark face, or should that be a dark force, that she didn't like.

More importantly, it didn't like her.

CHAPTER FIFTEEN

The young couple went out into the town and had a meal at a restaurant that one of Laurel's friends had recommended. The girlfriend had been suitably jealous when introduced to Billy, and that made Laurel smile. According to Laurel, the girlfriend, Karen, had gone into hospital for a knee operation and had come out with a bigger pair of boobs.

Laurel continued to share information on her life story in snippets, all of which Billy gladly took in and offered little in return. Not because he didn't want to share but just that there was nothing to share. Billy really didn't have much to share. It was only when he was recalling the Big Events of his life that he realised just how empty his years had been. It was just one more thing to make Billy wonder just how it was he'd gotten her.

They took a long, relaxed stroll through the city, Billy quite happy to be reduced to nothing more than a hot-ass piece of man meat. Laurel didn't actually call him a hot-ass piece of man-meat, but that was the general idea. Everyplace they went, they bumped into someone that Laurel know, and Billy was paraded in front of them.

'Are you sure you wouldn't prefer me in a pair of skin-tight short-shorts?' he asked jokingly.

'Later,' Laurel replied. 'We have places to go.'

***

The night was still, the air was stifling. Laurel was asleep in the bed, next to Billy, naked and glistening both. She really was just too perfect. He felt a light pulsating in his head and so went to the kitchen to get a glass of water.

That woman's dehydrated me. Thank you, God!

On his way to the kitchen he felt a slight breeze, and still half asleep and absent minded went into the painting room to close the window. Once he got in there, he noticed the window was already closed. He turned and saw that the easel was already set-up, there was a fresh canvas in place, and paint was already supported in a pallet.

Billy's headache grew, his penis twitched as though at the start of an erection, but then decided to remain limp. In some distant thought Billy wondered if he'd damaged it. The pulse in his brain grew so strong it was almost echoing through his skull. In blurred, slow motion, he started to paint, his every movement leaving vapour trails before his face. He was vaguely aware of the colours he was putting together in front of him, but remained clueless to the shapes they were forming.

Behind him, stood watching like a guard or disciplinarian, Billy was aware (but carefree) of the Japanese man looking on.

Then Billy could feel liquid oozing its way down over his lips and dripping off his chin. The nose bleed felt heavier than ones he'd experienced before.

Then, Billy zoned out.

He was in that state for maybe four hours or so before Laurel woke up in the bed, and after waiting several minutes for Billy to return from wherever it was he'd gone to, decided to go looking for him. As wonderful a time as she'd had earlier in that bed, being alone in it was just creepy. She decided it was probably best to put the lights on, and wore a blue t-shirt of Billy's, as she didn't feel comfortable snooping about in his flat in the nude.

'Billy?' she called. 'Billy? You there?'

It was her first call of his name that released the grip of whatever Dark Force held him in the paint room, causing him to collapse to the floor unconscious. He lay motionless on the floor, crumpled paintings beneath him, blood drying on the top of already dried blood that had dyed his upper-lip crimson.

Laurel heard the thud of Billy's well-built body hitting the floor and rushed to the room, only realising where she was going once she'd entered and was three rushed, and suddenly halted, paces inside. Against her prehistoric instincts to run or curl up into as tiny a ball as she could, Laurel stood her ground and began reaching out both arms in search of the walls like a blind man without a cane. At last, after what felt like an age, she placed her left hand on the wall and began to feel along like a drunkard stumbling home.

She found the small white plastic square she was looking for and turned the light on, illuminating Billy's prone body. The first thought that ran through her mind quick as a lightning bolt was that Billy was dead, she was sure of that, no two ways about it. This was quickly followed by a shriek of terror as she knelt down to the body and saw it rise with shallow breaths. After leaping back and bringing her hand to her mouth, she let her pulse slow back down to a steady, healthy pace. Right up the centre of her body she felt very light, as the adrenaline rushed through he system.

There were times when an adrenaline rush was second only to an orgasm in the all-time great feelings.

Finally composing herself, Laurel knelt down on the rough carpet and shook Billy, waking him.

'Laurel,' he said. 'What's wrong?'

'You're asking me what's wrong?'

'Of course, yeah.'

'Billy, sweetie, you're on the floor in your paint room.'

'I am?'

'Yes.'

'Oh...why?'

Laurel explained that she didn't really know why Billy was asleep on the floor on the other side of the (admittedly small) apartment, but that he might have injured himself because his nose, mouth and chest were caked with blood. She pointed with a trembling finger at the blood, Billy almost cranking his neck trying to look down at his own chest.

'I suppose a quickie is out of the question?' he smiled.

Helped and stabled by Laurel, Billy climbed to his feet on not completely steady legs. He stood there, their bodies pressed close to each other he warmth felt very good against his skin, as the prolonged exposure had lowered his temperature considerably. He stood and smelled her hair, and kissed her head.

Laurel didn't notice.

Her eyes were dead ahead on the easel. Transfixed on the images Billy had been painting from his subconscious. The pictures of diabolical perfection that Billy knew he was responsible for, but no matter how hard he tried he'd never recall committing to canvas.

'Billy it's...it's so...oh,' Laurel said, clearly overwhelmed by the vision she saw. The clarity, the perfection. The realism of the art work standing before her. Her eyes huge and wet. Her words choked in her throat.

Billy saw what he'd been painting during the night.

It was the most accurate and detailed portrait of Laurel he'd ever done. She was looking out at him with a bright orange haze behind her, but the paint only took up a small amount of space in the centre of the page. A shiver ran up Billy's spine, he knew the painting wasn't finished yet, and worried about what might be added to it at a later date.

'Oh, you're cold,' Laurel said rubbing Billy's back.

'Yes.'

No, he thought. Not cold. Scared.

***

Billy found it hard to sleep, his mind racked with terrifying thoughts. He'd started painting again. Painting Laurel again. Although she seemed to be in a good mood in the picture, and she had what he presumed to be some type of sunset behind her, he knew it wouldn't be good. He refused to allow himself to believe it would come to good.

(Maybe it's not a sunset, maybe it's nuclear fallout?)

Billy would gladly pay for years and years of therapy if it meant that voice, the Voice of Reason, would stop in his head.

Whatever he added to the painting, he knew it wouldn't be something he would like. He thought that perhaps it wouldn't be that bad, because Laurel is still alive in the picture. What the hell could it be? He asked himself. Maybe there was a way to prevent it? Maybe Billy could go into the painting room once the sun was up and finish the picture off when he was aware of what he was doing? Whatever magic it was at work that controlled the painting, it had to be stopped.

Billy had a sense, a very strong sense that no, it couldn't. It could not and would not be stopped. It couldn't be reasoned with, it couldn't be bargained with. It would continue to go on and on until its purpose had been fulfilled. It had something to do, had some reason to be here, and it wouldn't go away until it had finished its business.

CHAPTER SIXTEEN

Four weeks went by without Billy painting. It was true that he'd mainly accomplished this by staying at Laurel's place as much as he possibly could, and working long hours at the gym, but still, he did manage to lay-off the paints for a month. When he wasn't at work or with Laurel, the key was to stay out of his home as long as he could. This resulted in a massive increase in his running, at one point managing 100 miles a week. He dropped eighteen pounds that he never really had to lose, giving him a very sculpted, cut look. He did occasionally look ill, but never as ill as he felt.

The runs around town were deplorable. The views were non-existent, he breathed in nothing but fumes, the concrete didn't do his knees or ankles any good, and due to people and traffic he was never really able to break into a decent rhythm, never able to let his mind wonder away from the troubling thoughts that had plagued him for so long. Constantly he felt the weight on his shoulders of this, this curse? This burden? This gift? Whatever it was, its presence was always felt at every moment of his waking life.

Billy would occasionally think he could smell paint, but he shook those thoughts out of his mind. It was, he supposed, nothing more than when he'd been sat curled up with Laurel on her sofa at night and he was sure he could feel a paint brush between his fingers. It was his brain telling him to go again, calling him to paint once more, like the needle calls out to a junkie. The power of whatever it actually was continued drawing him nearer, always beckoning to him, calling from afar.

You need me, it whispered to him in the quiet times.

You want me, the soulless, gravely voice whispered to him during the lonely periods.

He found it difficult to eat. He had trouble sleeping. The paintings, the blank canvas on the cold easel, the last, unfinished painting of Laurel, was always on his mind. Always hovering with crystal clarity just before his eyes everywhere he went. With a sick, perverted chuckle, Billy had to admit to himself that although he was running away from this dark, powerful force, he was actually exhibiting the call-signs of love. Love. Love for the power he had, but could not control? Love of creation? Maybe there was an almost orgasmic feeling during the actual event of painting, but it was long-gone by the time he woke up the next morning.

Billy didn't know, but then he figured you didn't need to be familiar with the technicalities of osmosis to know when it was pissing it down on you.

The more Billy attempted ways to remove himself from the surroundings and trappings of the paintings, the more the urge called to him. The greater he pulled away, the greater the paints and the brushes and the canvases pulled him in. On the few occasions that he went back to his apartment, he could feel a tug, a wrench in his stomach whenever he passed the permanently closed door to the paint room. The veins in his neck stood out like cords, his muscles tensed and sweat left a sheen on his skin every time he passed that door. The iron taste of blood came up in the back of his throat, the first few times leading Billy to believe he was about to vomit, but the feeling went away once he was clear of that doorway, clear of that room.

At times Billy was almost able to put it out of his mind, to get the images of the paintings out of his thoughts, but just as soon as the thought came that he was no-longer under the ill-pressure that forced him to crate these images. All at once a billion of his pictures flashed across the big screen in his head, bringing with it the thick urge to vomit.

Once he'd sat down, alone, under the grey sky on a park bench that over-looked the town, and he tried to work it all out. He'd come up here a few times, high above the city, because it was a hard slog to get up this high and very few people knew about it. Billy often thought that the city appeared had he been seeing it through a grey cloth. Always looking as if it were about to pour with rain, or perpetually smog-covered.

Behind him ran a man, well-built, Billy recognised him as a bouncer at one of the night clubs in the city centre, Angles he thought it was. Billy had spotted the man a handful of times before, the man would then disappear up and over the hills behind the park, popping up once in a while, smaller with each passing peak as he further and further away from the park.

'Hill sprints,' Billy said softly to himself. In a previous life, hill sprints had been the hardest thing Billy had to deal with.

But that was a life before the paintings.

CHAPTER SEVENTEEN

'You're here then?'

Laurel's voice cracked through the boundaries of slumber and woke Billy from his dreamless sleep on the sofa in Laurel's living room. For the first second awake he didn't know where he was. He was just happy not to smell paint. Once his mind cleared and remembered where he was, he realised it was Laurel, the beautiful woman in his life, he was talking to.

'Sorry,' he began. 'What?'

'I just saw Ash from the gym, he was wondering where you were?'

'Well I'm here, aren't I?'

'I can see that, can't I?' she joked, putting a bag of shopping down onto the coffee table. 'Only you were supposed to be at the gym.'

'Was I?'

'Yes,' she said as she leant forward and placed a kiss on Billy's lips.

'Oh, of course.'

Billy rolled of the couch, a noticeable twang in his left calf as though he'd pulled it somehow. Must be getting old, he thought. Never pulled a muscle in my sleep, before.

He also felt a low, dull ache in both shoulders and traps, as if he'd been carrying a very heavy bag, and the straps had been digging into his flesh and muscles. He brought up a hand to rub the sore muscles, wondering if he'd maybe slept awkwardly on the couch, even though he couldn't remember any other times when he'd woken up on the sofa with such aches in the past. Having said that, Billy could also usually remember getting onto the couch to go to sleep...all he could remember now was, well, not a lot if he was truthful.

As Laurel took the bag of shopping into her bedroom, she called back to Billy about the stat of the spare room. The spare room? What spar room? Billy couldn't recall the spare room, had no memories of there ever even being a spare room.

'What spare room?' Billy quizzed, still half asleep and very confused.

'The spare room,' came Laurel's reply.

'Oh, well now that you've repeated it.'

'The room next to my bedroom. It's a good job you've got that body because your brain is mush.' Laurel joked expecting a witty retort. It never came, prompting her to ask aloud with more than just a slight quiver of fear in her voice for her man. 'Billy? Billy? Bill?'

Laurel exited her room and went back into the sitting room. All she found was a sneaker that had been dropped carelessly on the floor. It was splattered with paint. Carrying the shoe in her hands, its paint-assaulted laces hanging down loosely, Laurel made her way back to her room. She stopped dead in her tracks when she heard Billy at work in the spare room. 'Billy?' she muttered, annoyed that he hadn't answered her but at the same time relieved that he was, or at least appeared to be, okay.

CHAPTER EIGHTEEN

Laurel walked into the spare room, which only just was capable of being called room, and was shocked at what she saw. Billy was slumped on the floor, dead.

'No!' she screamed at tears streamed down her face, she wanted to rush forward but her feet were stuck to the spot. All at once more thoughts ran through her mind than ever before in her life. She wondered why he would leave her, why he had to die, why would the fates bring him into her life just to be ripped out again.

'Don't shout,' Billy said with a wince.

He was still alive! Laurel quickly thanked any and all gods that might be watching as she hurled herself down on top of Billy and kissed his face repeatedly, and then kissed him deeply, lolling her tongue about inside his mouth,

'I thought you were,' she had difficulty getting the words out through her tears. 'Why are you on the floor if you're not...'

The sobbing broke her sentence again.

'My leg fell asleep, so I took the weight off it.'

Again moving her mouth as if to speak, no words came out, and Laurel slapped Billy on the shoulder. He held her tightly, whispering in her ear that it was okay, everything from now on was going to be okay, it was going to be absolutely fine. As Billy said this, he looked up over Laurel's shoulder. The Japanese man dressed in the long robe was stood in the door way, looking around the room at the walls. He stared with great contemplation at what he was seeing.

'It is going to be okay now, isn't it?' Billy asked looking at the Japanese man.

The Japanese man inhaled deeply, this was not the type of judgment call to make on a whim.

'Of course it will,' Laurel said. 'Of course it will, of course it will.'

Billy looked to the Japanese man, who finally made eye contact. He nodded, slowly, once and then was gone.

Billy had never been so relieved in all his years.

'Laurel, honey, look at me,' he said breaking the hug and pushing her back.

'What? What is it?' she asked with more than just a little worry in her voice.

'Look. Look.' Billy urged Laurel to inspect the room.

The walls were covered in large square canvases, all joined together up and down and across the walls, pieced together to form one giant, floor-to-ceiling mural. Even the small window had been covered up. The light from the window behind helping to give it a special effect to the canvas that covered it. Laurel saw herself, stood in a cream dress, strapless, that was pushing up and making the most of her ample cleavage. Although there was no indication, Laurel thought, quite correctly, that she had been painted in her wedding dress. She looked beautiful, a gorgeous sun was shining behind her, and she'd never looked happier.

The rest of the mural that stretched out across all the walls depicted the rest of the world, all the various lands, countries, religions, races, creeds, sexual orientations were represented. Upon closer inspection, Laurel could also see that they were all smiling, all absolutely in love with each other.

It made her happy to look at, filled her with a warmth deep inside.

'What is this?' she asked with wide-eyed wonder.

'What does it look like?' Billy said getting to his feet. Laurel stood in silence, slowly shaking her head in amazement. Billy put an arm around her said, 'It's world peace, honey. We did it.'

And then leaned in to kiss her.

JAUN VEGA

Look, I can't exactly tell you why it all happened, and I know that on the surface of things I come across as the slutty little whore who cheated on her husband, but I had my reasons. I think. Again, I'm not exactly sure, it's confusing even to me, still, so if I lose my train of thought you'll have to forgive me. Or don't. I haven't precisely forgiven myself for it yet. I'm not entirely convinced that I did anything that needs to be forgiven.

I can tell you the moment I cheated on my husband, for the

first time, it was three weeks ago and although it was quick it was also exhilarating, passionate, and life-affirming. Odd, really, that sex with a stranger should be thought of as life-affirming, but it was. I don't know if ti was just because he was someone different or because we could have been caught or because his cock was the thickest God-damn thing I've ever had in my mouth, but it made me feel sexy and wanted and desirable for the first time in a very long time. But I'm getting ahead of myself. To tell you this properly I need to tell you all of it, every little (and every not-so-little) detail.

We'd been married, Stewart and I, for three years. He was, and is, a nice man. No complaints there. He's never beaten me, never really yelled at me, never cheated on me (to the best of my knowledge) and is a good provider. He has a very good job with a law firm and we have a wonderful home. He's safe. The problem with all of that, as you might guess from my tone, is that he's, well....safe. There comes a time when a woman wants that, she needs that; security is a very important part of life.

But...

But it should always be at the back, under the surface. You know when you're on a roller-coaster that you're not really going to be shot-off and be launched into the abyss of the unknown or suddenly dropped a hundred feet to your death, but you can put that knowledge away and enjoy the thrill of the ride. That's what I wanted from life, from relationships, from my marriage.

What I got was boredom. Every fourth morning, like clockwork, we have sex. And I mean like clockwork, too. On the small bedside calendar on Stewart's side he has every fourth day marked with a tiny little 's' in the top right corner. Fitting, really, that it might be a tiny little one. Actually, no, that's too hard on him. He's roughly average, which is fine. And of course, when we first got together he was new, which was good, and when you fall in love with someone size isn't important, and back then Stewart really put in the time, before his idea of foreplay was looking at the calendar, giving me a nudge and saying, 'Oh, it's time.'

No, really, let me tell you. I have to. You have to see how passionate he was at the beginning. I think it'll help you see how far we'd fallen by that part, which should, if you have any compassion at all, help you understand why I cheated on him. Why I had to cheat on him.

At the start he was incredibly charming. We met at a friend's birthday dinner. Everyone looked so amazing that evening; Samantha had turned thirty-five, she was making a very big deal about being fine with it leading us to believe that perhaps she wasn't as okay with it as she wanted us to believe. Her home was a large, open-planned sprawling place that was never going to feel as warm and comforting as a home should feel, but it put my apartment at the time to shame. Anyway, knowing that Samantha knew some pretty important people, I made an effort to look my best; tight little black dress that clung to my hips like a second skin and showed off my ass spectacularly, if I do say so myself. I wore a pair of classy black heels that I always thought made my legs look a little longer (though I'm 5'7, I'm not exactly a munchkin), and was ready to let my thighs do the flirting.

You see, back then I didn't have these. I was pretty much flat and most days I only ever bothered with a bra if I wanted to wear one of those expensive lacey ones I had to make myself feel sexy. No, Stewart bought me my C-cups as an engagement present (an believe me, the amount of friends and co-workers who told me that should have been a warning sign was unreal).

So, the dinner itself I don't really remember, what I do recall with clarity, however, was that Stewart wouldn't hear of me getting a taxi and drove me home himself. Not really one for cars, I can't tell you what type it was, but I can tell you that it was several hundred grand's worth of automobile, and it made Stewart a lot sexier somehow. It was only after we moved in together that he confessed it was a company car and that he was a long-way off being reckless enough with cash to spend that much on a car.

Look, the car wasn't the important part of the story, what we got up to was.

It was already close to midnight when we pulled into the dark car park at the back of my building. None of the windows on that side had any lights on, which didn't necessarily mean no one was up, just that they were doing whatever in the dark. I was about to do the same.

'Can I ask you something?' he'd said then. He'd shifted in his seat to look at me better, and if I'm honest, yes I really wanted him to lean in and kiss me.

'If you want,' I said, as coyly as I could muster. Don't get me wrong, I can usually flirt with the best of them, but there was just something different here. I knew that whatever this was, it was going to be a lot more serious than just a lift home and a peck on the cheek.

'How is it you're single?'

I'd be lying if I said I wasn't flattered at that, but then that was the point, wasn't it? I blushed, and seductively bit at my lower lip, something that always drove men wild. Before I had the chance to gather my thoughts and plan my next move (how to let him know I'm available but not come across as easy?), his after-shave filled my head and he was kissing me. It was a soft, tender kiss at first, as kiss I've always thought of as romantically classy. Then it changed. The pressure increased, I felt his teeth gently grip onto my lower lip (I guess I made it look quite appealing) and his hand, strong and firm, slid slowly from the side of my head, between my breasts, and teasingly along my inner thigh. I'm a little embarrassed to admit this, but I got moist far quicker than I should have.

Maybe it was just because I'd been single for a while, or perhaps it was because I was able to completely give-up control to someone else. That release of responsibility, to totally be, not dominated but to not have to care about what's going on, to just give in to the moment.

Stewart's mouth moved from my lips, onto my chin, and then along my jawbone. I think it was a combination of being single for so long, as I mentioned, and him knowing exactly what he was doing, but it was amazing. He blew hot breath gently into my ear before biting my lobe and sending me crazy. His fingers slid up and rubbed gently on the warm wetness he found. He kissed down my neck as his fingers burrowed under my panties and pinched to pull lightly at the little tuft of hair I keep down there. Nobody had ever done that before, and the tingling sensation it sent like a lightning bolt through my groin was a most welcome feeling.

I turned my face to him fully and he kissed me, his tongue probing with just the right force, he took my hand in his spare (the other hand was still obscured form view and caressing my pussy lips), and placed my palm on the crotch of his trousers, and I was startled to feel just how hard he was. I have to admit it was more than just a little flattering to think I had that effect on him.

He moved those fingers into me, probing and moving and wriggling and doing exactly what needed to be done. I can't quite put it in the right words for you, but a big part of the pleasure was the taboo. Now don't get me wrong, I'm no prude but giving and receiving some hand time in a car outside an apartment building, knowing that any number of eyes could be on us from those darkened windows, staring down on us, made it so naughty and exhilarating. Just briefly it flashed through my mind that maybe there was another couple up there, in one of those windows, getting up to no-good like we were just there in the car.

After what seemed like no time at all, I reached orgasm. It wasn't the most explosive, but Stewart's fingers roaming within me and his thumb hitting my clit just right did the job. It was only after I snapped my thighs together, essentially trapping his hand, poor baby, that I relaised my hand was sticky. Stewart had come in his trousers, the fabric there now sporting a wet patch.

We remained, foreheads touching, and breathing deeply, like that for a few moments, until the dampness of our crotches became irritable. We said our goodbyes, and I got myself home and showered and changed. Over the next few weeks myself and Stewart grew closer, and slowly stopped being so paranoid every time I saw someone who lived in my building, and within two months we'd spilled out the 'I Love Yous' and by the end of the first ten months we were living together. Did we rush into things? Probably. Did we get married too soon? Yes, we did. We were in love, madly and stupidly, but we should have waited. If we were so sure we were going to spend the rest of our lives together then we should have been okay putting the wedding off for a year or two.

But of course we didn't wait. We rushed in, fuelled by love. And love will make you do the dumbest things.

2

Now I don't know how well-travelled you are, or how well you know your geography, but I for one would never pick Geography and World Travel as my specialist subjects, so it should come as no surprise that when Stewart placed the airline tickets in front of me on the glass kitchen table I had no clue at all of where Juan Vega was. It turns out it's a small tropical island off the Bahamas, that is available only to the very wealthy or the very well connected (and luckily by this point in our lives we could confidently claim to be both), and boasts some of the most luscious-looking beaches you could dream of. Long stretches of pure, fine, white sand, lapped at gently by clear, turquois seas. When stewart showed me the images on Google the excitement to get out there grew.

The problem here was this; only a year or so before Stewart would have made a big deal out of presenting me with the gift, at the very least he would have held me from behind and made me close my eyes. Not the lifeless dropping of the tickets without a care, nearly landing in my half-a-grapefruit. Unceremoniously was never a word I, or anyone I knew, would choose to describe a relationship, let alone a marriage. I can't speak for you or anyone other than myself, but from my point of view I, as a woman, as a wife, as a human in love, would like to not be thought of as comfortable, which is actually what the marriage had become. Comfortable. Safe. Boring, Dull.

Packing was simple enough, even with the limited knowledge I had of Juan Vega based on the pictures I'd seen and what little Stewart had told me (leading me to believe that his own knowledge of the place wasn't that much more than mine), I knew my Louis Viton case was going to filled primarily with bikinis (part of me was looking forward to seeing how Stewart would react to seeing the twins, as he called them, on display again), an evening dress or two and a selection of footwear (and remembering some very sound advice, a comfortable pair of flats).

The flight out was as uneventful as could be, soave for one incident. I was, in my fantasy dream trip scenario, hoping that there would be some square-jawed male flight attendant who would flirt shamelessly and make me feel wanted and make Stewart feel a bit jealous. Nothing like that happened. Most of the cabin crew were, not to be down on them, but they were… shall we say unfortunate-looking? Anyway, there's a reason those things are kept to fantasy.

About halfway through the flight, Stewart's hand rested on my knee. After a quick moment, he gave my leg a squeeze. I thought, rather naively I see now in retrospect, that the tropical surroundings might ignite something in him. His hand slid further up my leg, which caused me some embarrassment as it was two in the afternoon and broad daylight and everyone on the plane could see and this wasn't a car in a darkened carpark. He leant close to me and whispered into my ear and revealed something I genuinely never knew about him or would ever have thought about him.

'I want you right now,' he breathed heavily in my ear. 'In the bathroom. How about it?'

Honestly, I was as close to disgusted by my husband as

I'd ever been. I mean, this was supposed to be a romantic long weekend, it was going to revamp our lagging sex life, and Stewart wanted us to go at it in the toilet. The toilet. The worst, least-sexy smell in the universe, and combined with the possibility of putting your foot in a pool of blue chemicals, who could say no? Me, that's who. I took Stewart's hand in mine rather than just pushing it away from my leg, and told him that no, we wouldn't be engaging in that activity in that room. It would be better to wait until we got to the hotel.

Seriously, for the rest of the journey, he sulked like a child. I made up my mind to not let it get to me and that once in the hotel room I'd make up for it. When we first started seeing each other there was a special little thing for him when giving a blowjob. Now I'm not going to bore you with all the silly details about kissing down his body and teasing him and kissing his inner thighs, but I'll get straight to the point; once he was hard and his cock was glistening I'd flick my tongue on the inverted V at the back of his helmet. I'd vary my tempo and swap the flicks for long, slow licks, but in each case it got him off in not time at all. This was back in the days when oral sex was still on the agenda and our foreplay involved more than crossing a day off the calendar.

I truly felt like I was going to burst with sexual desire, and the quicker we landed and got to the hotel the better, but there was no was at all I was going to be working the cock in a toilet.

3

The hotel was gorgeous. It was all smooth marble in reds and white and creams, and it was spacious and gave the impression that absolutely anything was possible in life. The idea that the people who worked there were probably bored of the place brought a chuckle from my throat, but then I knew that anyone could get bored of anything, regardless of how thrilling it had been at the beginning.

I can't really recall too much about the foyer or the rest of the hotel, and I can't really imagine that you care too much about those details, either. What I can tell you is that the moment we were in our luxury apartment, we were at each other's clothing, buttons and zips and laces be damned. I got his shirt and his shoes off, and then pushed Stewart back and onto the bed, straddled him, and placed little kisses onto his bare skin and began to slide my way down his body. My beautiful manicured nails (yes, I'd made sure to have them done before we left) left little white lines on his skin as I dragged them over his torso. Back when we met, Stewart had jogged three times a week and spent an hour a day on weights and push-ups and sits-up. Those days were long-gone, but still, it hadn't been only his body I'd fallen for.

My hands worked expertly and unbuckled his belt with minimal fuss as I circled his bellybutton with my tongue, which was something that always revved my engine when he did it to me, and it seemed to have the same effect on him. I pulled his sensible dress pants off, and was pleased to see the miniature Eiffel Tower threatening to burst loose from his light grey boxers, only a tiny dark spot at the tip of his penis breaking up the blandness of his underwear.

Before I had the chance to take them off and take him in my mouth, he had sat up and, rather too calmly for my liking, unzipped my summer dress and shimmied me out of it, and pulled off my lace panties, but left my matching bra on. That, I thought, I was quite curious. He kissed me, used the flat of his fingers to lightly slap at my vagina, and then entered me. I gasped, as I wasn't quite as wet I wanted to be, but I soon got, if not quite back to where I'd be on the plane then close enough. The passion, the urgency had built up, and then....

And then...

Shrug. Shrug-shrug. Shrug-shrug.

To say I was bored would be wrong, but we weren't exactly revolutionising sex. I was actually able to concentrate, not just think, mind, but to really concentrate fully on what bikini-sarong-shoe combo to debut first. Look, I don't know if Stewart thought this was amazing sex or if he knew it was just perfunctory, but I suppose it doesn't matter. Not really. His rhythm never varied; slowly at first then picking up the pace before slowing down again to make thigs last before one quick, last surge that would take him over the edge. His right eye always twitched closed when he comes, and his face contorts and it's really all I can do to look away or bote into his shoulder to suppress the laugh.

He placed the same gentle kiss on the corner of my mouth that he always does after, and then I watched with longing as his pale, shapeless buttocks, danced their way to the ensuite bathroom. I wished then for a holiday romance. For an affair, for a three-way, for a gang-bang, for anything that would make this, this, bearable for the rest of my life.

Careful what you wish for.

I rose, and moving quicker than I usually did because I was naked, rummaged through my bag and pulled out a two-piece blue bikini that, if I do say so, made my ass and my tits pop. I finished the ensemble with a pair of cork-heeled mules and opened the balcony doors that looked out over the small U-shaped courtyard at the front of the hotel. I was expecting a view of the beach, a view of the ocean, the clear blue sky. I saw something else, but, oh my, it was a view all the same.

To my left, no more than a hundred feet away on another balcony, was who I consider to be the most beautiful man have ever seen. He was tall, and tanned, long raven black hair that he wore loose about his broad, muscular shoulders. He had the perfect six-pack that you usually only find on underwear models, except he was completely naked, and, although his penis wasn't huge by any means (certainly it was closer to his balls than his knees), it was perfect. It was hanging low enough to be distracting, and it had some girth even when it was sleeping, the whole package was…beautiful. I don't know if anyone's ever described a cock as beautiful before, but this one most certainly was.

I hadn't noticed, but my nipples had grown into two tight,

hard pebbles, clearly visible as though trying to burst through the blue fabric of my bathing top. I'd been thinking, concentrating, on that beautiful man, and on the feeling he was causing in my pussy. I also hadn't noticed that he had turned and was looking straight at me. I raised my gaze north of his naval and he had the most charming smile I'd ever seen. He flashed his white, straight teeth at me, waved his hand, and then stood, legs apart and hands on hips as if to frame and thrust his package at me and say, yeah, check this out.

Blushing, and feeling the heat on my face bring out a fresh clamminess on my brow, I darted back into my room. Judge me if you must, but at that moment, had I not heard Stewart turning the shower off, I would have been down the hallway looking for that beautiful man's room.

'Hey honey,' Stewart said to me as he left the ensuite, the towel over his head, his naked, pudgy body completely exposed. He saw my flushed skin and my erect nipples and grinned. I could tell by the shrivelled member sat atop his balls however that round two for us was going to have to wait.

4

At no point did Stuart tell me exactly why we were at the Juan Vega resort until we saw the silver-haired, almost orange with tan man who is his boss at the law firm. It seems there was a considerable amount of networking to be done that night, and there was. If I was hoping that this trip was going to stave off boredom, I was going to be let down. We had dinner that night, with two of Stuarrt's co-workers and the Silver Fox, each of those men with accompanying bimbos young enough to be their daughters. You know what goes great with boredom? Alienation. The old man boss paid more attention to me than Stuart did, but at least when my hubby looked at me he looked at more than just my cleavage.

To say I wasn't in the best of moods when I was dragged along to some darkened night club would be a slight understatement. But I was and I went, and I'm a grown woman and nobody really forced me to go, so I have to take responsibility for going, and for everything that happened when we got there.

I have a limit to how much I can take of drunken, inane ramblings and so just under an hour after getting there I excused myself to go powdered my nose (and what a ridiculous saying that is in a night club). I stood in that night club bathroom, the effort put into decorating that room made it several grades better than all else I'd seen in that club, and stared at myself for a good long while. I didn't know where my head was at, or what I was doing there, but I did know that happily married women didn't have their heads all over the place like mine was then.

'Get a grip, Krista girl,' I told myself. I checked my make-up, reapplied some lip gloss, and went back out with the full intention of giving Stuart a hand job under the table. I was going to make him remember how amazing I was and that there was still a sexual spark between us.

Entering the large main room, I saw the at the far side of the light-up dance floor, Stuart and the rest of our party dancing like drunken dummies. I stood in the shadows, nobody else around me, and I watched on. I don't know if I ever felt more alone than I did right then. Before I could get sad enough to cry, a very strong arm wrapped itself around my waist like a boa constrictor encircling its prey. In a way, I was prey. I don't know who he was, I never got a look at his face, but as his muscular forearm draped itself across my midsection, he peppered my neck with gentle yet hungry kisses and breathed heavily in my ear. I'll be honest here and tell you that the outside world stopped then; only myself and this mystery man existed.

I didn't try to stop him, I didn't try to turn around to look at him, I was just happy for him to keep going. Within a matter of moments I could feel his hardness against my leg, and even without seeing it I knew that it was impressive. I found out soon enough. While his tongue lapped at my ear and hit teach gently bit my lobe, his penis slid into my hand. I'm glad it was only a hand job I gave him then, because it was the thickest one I've ever felt. I couldn't make my thumb meet my middle finger around it, though it was still a little bit squishy. I have heard that some of the truly big ones, the monsters, can't ever get fully hard. I guess that's true.

He didn't last overly long, maybe a few minutes, but I was well-aware that he shot out at least three good-sized loads, and I felt sorry for whomever it was that had to clean it up. He held me tightly, and I still kept a grip around his monster, even as it fell asleep and went flaccid, it was still quite the impressive specimen, making me think of a large, thick eel. I have to tell you that size was never an important part of the deal for me, but when personality and intelligence aren't part of the equation, there's just something about holding a massive member in your hand that really gets you going.

The man kissed me on the ear and left. I didn't look back, I preferred to keep it anonymous. The I did something odd. I could still see Stuart, dancing like an idiot, but decided my night was over. I left the night club and went back to the hotel. I felt grubby and dirty and just wanted to stand under a hot shower and scrub. I wanted to scrub away the hand job in the nigh club, I wanted to scrub away the thought of the beautiful man and his beautiful cock on the balcony, I wanted to scrub away the last few years of a dull marriage.

I didn't make it to my room that night.

5

Once in the hotel, I stopped by the elevators and sent Stewrat a text message, I didn't want him worrying about me, once he finally noticed that I wasn't there. Had I gotten on the elevator and sent the text from my room, things would have been different. I sent the message and then got on, just before the doors shut a man got on. He was wearing a cream-coloured jacket, white shirt, and baggy white trousers. He looked different, because his hair was tired back in a loose ponytail, but that smile was still drop dead gorgeous and the type that gets a girl in trouble.

'Hi,' he said. He had the most lyrical way of speaking, I can't really describe it as more than that.

'Hello,' I replied, blushing, and brushing the hair back behind my ear and trying not to make eye contact. I mean, what do you say in a situation like that? Lovely view from the balcony, you'r piece is a delight to behold, can't shake hands as I'm covered in some random guy's come?

'Good to see you again,' he said. That smile on his lips letting me know he wanted more than just a chat.

'I'm Krista,' I said extending my less-tired hand.

'Sexy name,' he answered, then leant in and kissed me. It was mostly a blur from there, but there was such a hunger in the man that I was as turned on as I've ever been in my life. He carried me from the elevator, my legs wrapped around his hips, one very strong and large hand cupped beneath my buttocks.

We burst into his room, the only light coming from the large balcony doors where he hadn't drawn the curtains. I was out of my dress and onto his bed in the blink of an eye. He was over me, his strength pinning me down, not that I had any intention of trying to get away. He kissed me and bit my tongue, my God, the first time that had happened and I hoped not the last. He kissed my neck, down along my collar bone and then kissed my breasts. He squeezed, perhaps a little too hard at first, one breast and pinched between his teach the hard nipple of the other through the bra fabric.

He kissed down my body, his finger tips tracing my ribs, before he nibbled gently at my hips. He continued kissing down, over the damp warmth of my panties, but instead of his probing tongue, I felt his lips moving down my inner thigh, coming to a rest to bite lightly at the inside of my knee. My legs seemed to have a life of their own, but he pinned them to the bed with strong hands, kissed down to my ankles, sucking on my toes as his fingers rubbed playfully on the outside of my panties. Oh, just fuck me now, I wanted to scream at him. He kissed back up my leg, and I hoped he wouldn't tease me by performing the same ritual on my other leg, and thankfully he didn't. He kissed back and forth across my pussy applying more and more pressure each time, before finally, finally, finally taking them in his teeth and pulling them off as his fingers raced across my body, stroking and caressing with perfect intuition.

Kissing through my pubic hair, he worked me up to a frenzy, before at last entering me with his tongue. He lapped like he was starving for me. A lot of men make the mistake of using only the tip of their tongue, but what really gets me going, and gets me off, is using the whole, long flat of the tongue. Lick me like you're eating an ice-cream cone and I'll be yours forever. He came out of me, kissed up my body to the bellybutton, and licked around it (that sends me crazy), and then licked down to my clitoris, which he circled with his tongue. At some point in all of this I lost my bra, which I wasn't aware of until I felt his hands squeezing my tits and then sliding my nipples between his fingers and teasing them. His lips took my engorged clit, and keeping wet rhythm, he made me cum so intensely that my cries must have woken up guests on the other side of the hotel.

My body, hyper-sensitive now, was still convulsing, I could feel the goosebumps on my skin, when he oved up torso and kissed me. The one and only time I've ever enjoyed tasting my own juices. Before I had the chance to reach down to him, he was sliding that beautiful hard cock of his into me. It was fairly impressive when flaccid, when fully engorged it must have looked down-right scary. He slid gently-but-firmly into me, and I was shocked at much girth I was feeling. I had never been filled up to that extent before, and I can't remember a time when the pain of being stretched was so pleasurable.

He slid in and out with such a gentle rhythm, lightly kissing my mouth and my neck before taking my nipples, each in turn, in his mouth and circling them with his tongue. He didn't just go straight for the hard pink buds, either. He kissed and licked all over my breasts before getting to the nipples.

I came twice more, my hips bucking up against him quite violently, before he finished. It was only when he came that I realised he wasn't wearing a condom. At the time that didn't worry me, not really. I didn't think he was diseased, and I didn't think I'd get pregnant (if you keep track of the days you can usually tell if you'll be okay or not, scare one for Stuart's stupid calendar). He pulled out, his massive cock flopping around like a large dead, drooling snake, and just stayed motionless at my side, gently kissing my shoulder. I can't remember if either of us spoke, I don't think we did, we just smiled at each other, got up, I got dressed, he was happy to walk around with his beautiful thing wrapping around, and I left.

Upon entry to the room I was relieved to see that Stuart wasn't back yet, which gave me the chance to shower, finally, and then climb into bed. I fell asleep pretty quickly, and it was the deepest, most refreshing sleep I'd ever had.

BLACK LEATHER

They all know what I do. They all look down their noses at me, call me names. Slut. Slag. Tart. Harlot. Tramp. Skank. Whore. The same women who call me those names are the ones married to men I know well. Very well.

Intimately well, you might say.

Black Leather, that's what they call me. I work nights, mostly. Usually lonely men, not always single men. Sometimes I get couples who want to spice things up a little bit. Sometimes I get gigs doing bachelor parties.

You ever play a game called smile? I have.

I sit all the guests at the stag night around a table, they each have a shot in from of them. I climb under the table and start to do 'things'. Those things could be playing with their balls, licking their dicks, rubbing their hard-ons with my tits, whatever. If the guy smiles, he has to take a shot. No one knows who I'll be giving my, ah-hem, attention to.

Sometimes my profession makes it onto the news. Should it be legalised? Should the porn industry be forced to adhere to prostitution laws? The answers, in case you're wondering, are yes and no, respectively.

Whatever you may think about what I do, take this into account, for a guy to approach someone like me, and to be willing to give me his cash in return for me getting him to come, he must really need it. Really, really need it. Need it to the point that a hard core DVD and a bottle of baby oil ain't cutting it for him no more.

When masturbation no longer does it for a man, then he's close to the breaking point, close to doing something nasty. Something evil. He's close to doing something to get what he needs, to get that feeling he needs. If he doesn't rent my talents, then he's likely to rape someone.

Every time I wipe someone's 'love' off my aching, leather-gloved arm, that's one less person raped.

Each time I feel someone shoot their load into the back of my throat, as their balls retract and shrink, that's one less person raped.

Any time I fake a synchronised orgasm, that's one less person raped.

Do you know, mine is the only profession that isn't police protected? It's true. Any other job on the planet, the police will look out for you, they're forced to look out for you, it's their job. A while ago I was beaten, pretty badly too. You see, the client refused to pay up, and so decided to give me a whooping to prove his point.

I'd have been mad to expect the police to have bothered with doing their jobs. They don't acknowledge my kind as people, we're dehumanised in the eyes of the law.

Just last week, a colleague of mine got raped. You know what happened when she went to the police? She got arrested for hooking. Does it seem fair to you that due to your line of work you're no longer protected by the police? Hell, even if you're a known bank robber or murderer, if you tell the police that you've been assaulted they'll at the very least look into it.

Judge me, and all my kind, as much as you want, but we're here, and we're all around and everywhere. We always have been and we always will be. Did you know that what I do is legal in Holland? Did you know that Holland has an almost non-existent rape percentage?

Think about it.

They call me Black Leather, and I'm very good at what I do. And what I do, is whatever you've got the cash for, honey.

Do you want my card?

<u>VIOLATED ANGEL</u>

The bright morning sun beams tear through the gap in the curtain, illuminating the tiny dust particles like incessant, angry fireflies. The room has an unnameable scent, a strange mixture of stale sweat, last night's whiskey and soiled prophylactics, thrown into a mound in the small metal bin.

As Howard wakes up, he is surprised. He drank enough whiskey last night to leave him with dramatic blank spots in his recollection of last night, but he figures he must've sweated it out between the late hours of last night and the early hours of this morning. But then, for all Howard knows, it could still be the early hours of this morning.

Claire looks like an angel. A beautiful, violated angel, wrapped in the red satin sheets which clutch to her curves like a second skin. A light sheen of sweat covers her body, and for a minute, a full sixty seconds, Howard truly believes that the violated angel beside him is aesthetic perfection.

Howard can still taste last night's cigarettes in his mouth, even though it was Claire who was smoking them, and a putrid stench of cigars from the fat business man in the hotel bar last night is still in his hair, reminding him again of how things got started.

It was by no means an accident that Howard and Claire were both in the hotel bar last night. They'd met at his law firm when she was hired as one of the partner's receptionist, and mutual attraction was instant and undeniable.

The affair had started, as millions have and do, at the office Christmas party, and just like the others, it hadn't ended there. The first thing Howard had noticed was her smile, but then almost in the blink of an eye he noticed her breasts.

Howard became fixated, often drawing sketches of what he thought her perfect breasts must look like, with hard erect nipples, or covered in baby oil and glistening or whipped cream or chocolate spread or whatever Howard's curious mind led him to think of.

Claire knew she was as damn-near perfect as any human could be, and often indulged her male co-workers by wearing low-cut tops, showing off her breasts that were as high-up, close to her shoulders as they could get without choking her.

Howard thought his chances were good, and all doubts were removed when he left the party to go to his office to get that special bottle of bourbon. He knew as soon as he started to open his office door that he'd been followed.

Claire followed Howard into the office, her intentions were obvious, painted on her face like a mask. Howard unlocked his cabinet, Claire refreshed her lipstick. He knew as he watched that it was for him and that the intentions were wrong, immoral.

What about his wife at home, sat up in front of the TV with their unborn daughter kicking inside of her womb? What about all the sacrifices she'd made? She'd been disowned by her own father for not marrying 'a nice Asian boy', and now he was seriously considering a one-night stand.

The contemplation didn't last long, as Claire bent over to pick up her dropped lip stick, exposing the tops of her hold-ups.

Howard used to believe himself to be a man of strong morals, but between just the right amount of alcohol in his blood system and Claire's figure-hugging red miniskirt were just too much to overcome.

There, in his office on the floor, they began their illicit sexually charged affair. It was an animalistic experience that Howard seemed to recollect hadn't been encountered sine he said his wedding vows three and a half years ago.

Of course, like all addicts and there addiction, once was never, ever going to be enough. What began as a once-a-week meeting rapidly turned into two or three times a week and had now evolved into spending nights together on what were laughingly being called 'business trips'.

Now, sat up in the bed, sharing his time between looking at Claire's perfect breasts and his watch, Howard was beginning to think they'd soon be caught. And now, as Claire was beginning to stir, Howard thought perhaps he wanted to be caught.

If he got caught, and all the sneaking about and lies and deception came to an end, then maybe the ulcers that were riddled throughout his 32 year old stomach would settle down and maybe even disappear. He'd no longer have to worry about calling his wife by the wrong name or wake-up in the middle of the night in a cold sweat afraid that he'd been talking in his sleep.

Of course, being caught would also mean ruining three lives.

Claire opened her eyes, and the steely blue piercing pools looked lost and weary. In that instant, Howard desperately wanted to hold and protect the woman who hours ago had been a savage beast, yet now looked like the most helpless, lost little girl in the world.

But then Claire sat up, leaving the satin sheet draped by her trim, taught waist, exposing her firm torso, and the reality that this was a fully grown woman hit Howard like a heavy weight boxing champion.

As Claire raised her arms high above her head as she stretched, Howard entertained thoughts of them 'being one' again, but his mind was racing and his body too sensitive and tired to do anything more than just sit there beside her.

'What time is it?' The words trembled over her full, cherry red lips.

'Just before nine' Howard checked his Rolex watch on the bed-side table.

The watch had been a gift from his parents on his graduating law school. Both mother and father proud that their little boy had grown up to be a man who just wanted to help people, at a nominal rate, of course.

As father presented son with the watch, he told of feelings of pride at how the fruit of his loins was making a career based on morals and ethics and doing the right thing. But that world was a lifetime away right now.

They both knew they should move. For one, their bodies are caked in a sticky, stale sweat. What little alcohol was in their systems is seeping slowly, almost oozing from their palms. Their breath is foul and harsh.

Claire makes a move first, but then stops suddenly and brings her legs back under the covers, right now very self con-scious about what she's determined to be her 'imperfect calves'.

'Silly bitch' thinks Howard. 'She's too stupid to even realise she's the perfect woman' Howard is sometimes too harsh on his perfect, violated angel. He also sometimes thinks he's just look-ing for things to hate about her so he can end it with her.

'We've got to make a move.' She's right. Howard knows she's right, he's been thinking the same thing. only, he knows as soon as he moves, as soon as one single muscle in his body so much as twitches, this moment will be over. Not that it's exactly a perfect moment. Not perfect like her.

Howard feels a strange sensation in hi chest. He really wants to lay back and enjoy this moment, with his perfect violated angel, but he's too nervous to. He's too anxious at the thought of being caught, and for Howard, anxiety isn't freedom. Maybe a cigarette would calm his nerves? Unfortunately, Howard's not the one who smokes. But Howard's sure Claire would be willing to teach him, she's taught him so much in the last 24 hours.

At the insistence of the naked angel, Howard rises form the bed, which for all intents and purposes is a satin draped tomb. For a moment Howard has difficulty getting his foot free from the blood-red sheets that have somehow managed to wrap themselves around his limb like a creeping vine strangling life from a tree.

Howard makes his way across the room to the en-suite bathroom, and his erotically burned out body is soothed by the coolness of the room. There's something disturbingly comforting about the sterile white walls.

Howard's hand reaches for the tap, but momentarily pauses as he thinks he hears Claire talking in the next room. He didn't. his mind's playing tricks on him. It always does when it comes to women, especially of the 'Angel' variety.

The cold water runs from the steel tap into the porcelain bowl, creating a magnificent pool of reflection. What it was reflecting was the face of a man committing adultery, possibly destroying a marriage. A man, if that's still the right word, who's doing his best to make a little girl be born into a broken home.

Howard cups the cold water to his face, in a vain attempt to wash away the guilt, wash away the sin. No matter how often the water splashes his face, no matter how hard he scrubs or wipes or washes, he knows what's always going to be staring back at him once the water settles.

One last time, Howard drenches his face and shuts his eyes. He shuts his eyes so tightly that for a few seconds he believes he can see the blood vessels running through the veins in his eye lids. He shuts his eyes so tightly that when he opens them again he sees dazzling sliver spots in the air.

And when the spots dissipate, Howard's left with nothing but his own, warn-out face. Howard can't help but smirk to himself at the thought. When the spots are gone, all that's left is Howard's worn-out self.

Claire follows Howard into the bathroom, only difference is she's wrapped in the satin sheets that Howard no-longer has a taste for since the bed grew arms and refused to give him his foot back.

'You gonna be long?' she asks him, her hip cocked to her right, exposing just enough thigh through the sheets to momentarily take Howard's attention off the question. She clutches the sheet to her chest, forcing her more than ample cleavage to take on a life of its own, damn near spilling out over the top of the make-shift robe. She's fucking with his head and he knows it.

Howard stands back from the basin, and stretches out his arm, signalling he's finished. Howard really doesn't rate Claire's intelligence. Maybe it's because she's a blonde with a huge chest, maybe it's because he's a chauvinist? Or it might just be the almost fifteen seconds that they were both stood back from the basin before Howard had to tell Claire he was done.

As Claire adjusts the sheet beneath her arm, her face contorts into a twisted shape that Howard's never seen before. Howard wasn't aware, didn't think it at all possible, for his angel to look this close to ugly. She's still not ugly, but she'd far closer than Howard ever thought he could be.

Claire reaches to the sink and pulls the plug out, condemning the water to the pipes of the hotel's plumbing system, where it will no-doubt be recycled and will probably be splashed into someone else's face in a bathroom just like this, before the week is out.

Claire looks absolutely disgusted that she has to reach her hand into the water to get the plug. These hotel plugs can't be found at the end of a chain, they've got a steel rod ensuring that they never leave the basin. I guess more people try to steal plugs than the TV.

Howard just doesn't get this crazy chick. Hours ago they were intertwined. Their bodies had melded into one sexually charged beast, writhing, contorting, flesh smacking flesh. Now, she won't even let him see her naked, and she's grossed out by having to come into contact with water he's just splashed on his face.

'Last night we had each other's genitals in our mouth, now she won't even touch water that ain't even dirty.' Howard really doesn't get women. His wife pulls the same crap at home.

His wife. Home. The torment was beginning to eat away at Howard's conscious like some lonely fat guy at a buffet. It was chomping through him like an unstoppable cancer. Howard hates this, all of it. Every last piece of this arrangement is clouded by hate, secrecy and jealousy.

As Claire dabs her wet hands over the beautiful, perfect contours of her face, Howard has what some would call mixed emotions. There's a part of him that wants to scoop Claire up in his arms, hide her away for himself and protect her from the outside world.

The other part of him just wants her to leave, to get the fuck out of his life, so he can go back to his pregnant wife and have the life he'd dreamt of since childhood. To be part of a family, built on love, not like his parents only ever seemed to argue about money.

'God' Howard thought, 'how much easier would all of this have been if Claire had been a prostitute?' Howard mulled this thought over as he watched Claire wash her face. And as much as he wanted to go, he couldn't help but think how good she'd look in that shower, the water cascading down the curve of her back, the droplets caressing her naked body.

Howard had one problem, though. He let his imagination run away with itself. He had no control over his mind and was totally unable to stop those thoughts. The thoughts of Claire being a prostitute filled his mind. Thoughts of her with different men, a different man each night. Hell, maybe even a different man each hour, after all, that's how they work.

Claire continued to chatter on about nothing, blissfully unaware that Howard was working himself into a frenzy. If she could've managed to take a step from her own little world for a second or two, she might have noticed Howard's face, a display of held-back rage and misplaced anger.

The beautiful, violated angel had a nasty little habit of getting talking and not shutting up about it until the next full moon. She had an annoying little history of running her mouth about her figure and not stopping until New Year's. And with her... charms, most men were happy to let her talk.

Howard's mind is not a happy place to be at the moment. All he can see is his beloved angel in satin writhing with other men, doing things to them and with them she'd never dream of doing with or to Howard. Or maybe what really angered him was the thought of another man doing things to her and with her that Howard couldn't.

Howard tried desperately to figure it all the hell out. How could she do that to him? Why would she be so cruel? After all he'd done for her in her career, after he'd risked his marriage, after he'd risked his family for her, how could she do this to him? Wasn't Howard enough for her? How could she do this to him?

Simply put, she wouldn't. Howard would see to that. Howard is determined not to ever let anyone get the better of him, that type of attitude is great in business, but not in relationships. Howard doesn't ever seem to be able to recognise the line between business and relationships.

If Howard did have the ability to separate the two areas then he probably wouldn't be thinking about Claire as though she were nothing more than a piece of property. If Howard was able to think rationally for even a minute then he'd have seen that he was acting foolishly.

'How easy would it be' Howard's thinking as he's trying to calm himself down by staring at Claire's perfect little ass, 'to just grab her head now and bounce it off the sink?' Now Howard's thoughts turn to how amazing the effect would be if Claire's blood were to be splattered through her blonde hair. The contrast, Howard decides, would be nice.

Howard's thoughts about killing Claire cease for just a moment. In that moment, Howard is thinking about that satin covered ass, and how it's perfect. It's not all fat and bulbous like so many female celebrities these days insist on having.

'Can you pass me the towel, please?' Claire's beautifully pitched voice breaks Howard's thoughts. Howard passes the white fluffy towel to his angel, and now he's thinking about how well the towel would work as both a silencer to muffle her screaming and a mop to soak up the blood.

Claire dabs the water from her face. Her face momentarily has a pinkish hue to it as the blood vessels get closer to the surface of the skin. Some of her nails still have a little bit of red nail varnish on them, last night it matched the colour of her lip stick. Now it matches the burst blood vessels in Howard's eyes.

Howard's pulse starts to race, his heart beating faster as he's thinking about killing the violated angel in front of him. Wafts of her perfume, faint as it is, still come to Howard's nostrils at undetermined intervals. And all it does I screw up Howard's fragile mind a little bit more.

He loves her. At least he thinks he does. Howard doesn't know what the hell he's thinking at the moment. One minute he wants to hold her in his arms and protect her, the next he wants to see her splattered across the bathroom tiles. Now Howard just wants it to be last night again.

Claire moves next door to the bedroom. She doesn't walk, she glides. She is elegance personified. She lets the red satin sheet drop gently to the bed from her perfectly manicured fingers. She moves over to the wardrobe and takes out the complementary dressing gown, which also is fluffy and white.

Howard stands, leaning on the door frame to the bathroom, just watching Claire move about the place. He could watch her for hours. And as soon as Howard has that thought, he immediately realises what he's doing. He's working himself into a rage, possibly in the hope that he'll get angry enough to end it with the angel in the white, fluffy robe.

Or, Howard thinks, maybe it's just a complete lack of faith and trust. Howard's cheating on a woman he has convinced himself he's still in love with, who also happens to be carrying a child he is sure he'll love. Only, he's cheating on her with another woman he is sure he is in love with.

So now Howard starts to think, 'If I'm cheating on a wife I love, what's to stop this magnificent angel cheating on me?' These thoughts are eating away at Howard like a carnivorous bacteria. Howard's pulse is getting stronger, his heart rate speeding up to a dangerous pace.

Claire is wondering around the room, looking for her other shoe. It's under the bed, but for some reason that's going to be the last place she'll look, or think of looking. Howard watches, and for a split second, he's wondering why his angel is looking for her shoes before the rest of her clothes.

Claire starts to rummage through her bag. The bag is nothing more than a sports hold-all, but last night in the midst of animalistic passion she stopped to move the damn thing like it was the most expensive piece of luggage that there had ever been.

The violated angel checks the side pockets. Why she's checking the side pockets is beyond Howard's powers of deduction. There is absolutely no way, not a single slither of a chance that her other shoe would fit in one of the side pockets of the hold-all.

Howard watches, and is disgusted by what he is now interpreting as her stupidity. 'Dumb bitch, she's probably forgotten what she's even looking for.' Howard is seriously trying to hate the woman who's made the last few hours bearable.

Claire pulls out a packet of cigarettes. She's still searching through the side pocket, and Howard knows what she's looking for. He walks across the bedroom to the TV, and picks up a silver lighter with James Dean's face etched onto it. He bought it for her as a gift, but she's a fan of Brando and Howard got them mixed up. Howard doesn't like films, and hates actors.

'Here.' Howard throws the lighter, and it swishes through the air like a silver star shooting through space. 'Thanks', Claire tries to catch the lighter, but she's got no hand-eye coordination to speak of, and James Dean lands face-down on the bed.

Claire picks up the silver fire-starter, and sits down on the bed. Howard can't help but think that there's something weird, something strange about this whole arrangement. What the hell I she doing with him? She could have any man on the planet, so why is she with Howard?

Howard has thought these thoughts before, but the thoughts about killing Claire are new, and Howard can't help but feel excited by these fresh thoughts. If he did kill her, then she'd be his forever, no other man could ever touch her, no one would be able to soil the purity of beauty.

She places the filter in her mouth, then pulls the rest of the cigarette packet away from her face. Howard has seen people take a cigarette out of the packet this way before, but it's never looked so erotic, so cool. So effortlessly cool. Mr. Dean on the lighter seems to smirk with pride.

Claire flips the lid, and with a roll of a thumb and flick of a spark there is a flame. The small, controlled ignited petrol illuminates her face as the flame is brought to the tip of the cigarette.

Howard despises cigarettes. He hates them. They have no

redeemable quality, no saving graces. He hates everything about them, the way they taste, the way they smell, the way they're making Claire's teeth yellow and causing lines to form on her upper lip. But at this moment, this precise moment in time, Howard wants to get on his knees and thank whichever God it was that created tobacco.

Claire exhales, breathing out smoke which appears to climb through the atmosphere of the room and disappears from view just before it reaches the ceiling. Howard absolutely hates the smell, that now mixes with the stale sweat, last night's cigarette butts, and used protection, to create a cocktail of smells that assaults the nostrils.

Howard moves quickly, first over to the bed with an ashtray from by the TV. Howard thinks of how easy it would be to just smash Claire several times in the head with it until she died. It's a big, heavy, thick-cut glass ashtray, with the hotel's emblem engraved on it. A few whacks with this and his problems would be solved.

Howard places the ashtray on the bed. He doesn't want to go through the hassle of trying to explain why he's being billed for burnt sheets to his wife. Howard tells his heavily pregnant wife that he's going on business trips, and that he needs to get a double room because he feels closed-in when he's staying in a single room, and claustrophobia buys his mind.

Of course, having to explain why a non-smoker was booked in a smoking room, and just how cigarette ash worked its way into the room and onto the bed would be very difficult. Howard doesn't think his wife would believe that one of the people he works with came to his room to call him for the meeting. Not that there was one.

Next Howard moves over to the window. Howard opens the curtains in the hope that letting in the daylight might make the room seem a little fresher. It doesn't.

Howard decides to open the windows, not that it'll make

much of a difference. In these hotels, the windows on the floors higher than the second only open six inches, in case someone should realise how pathetic their life is when they're alone during the night and decide to jump, resulting in their body plummeting to death. Higher than six, and the windows don't open at all.

As he looks out the window, Howard's thoughts turn to his wife, and his as-of-yet unborn child. Howard wanders if his child will grow up and have an affair. Howard wanders if his wife has had an affair. Howard wanders if his wife will have an affair. Howard tries to remember if his parents ever argued or split-up for a short time or ever fought when "another's" name was mentioned. Maybe if one, or both, of his parents had an affair then it would be easier to explain.

Maybe if he's genetically predisposed to committing adultery, then Howard won't feel as badly as badly as he does.

Now, suddenly, Howard's thoughts are interrupted. Claire is talking to him about something irrelevant, the colour of roses or why bees are called bees. And where did the "bumble" come from? Claire, as beautiful as she is, sometimes has a habit of talking about absolutely nothing of any worth for long periods of time.

'What do you think?' she's asked him that question a hundred million times before, and Howard has never known what to answer, primarily because he's always tuned out her voice before she can make a point.

'Well, what do you think?' This is Howard's stock response. Always. Whenever Claire asks Howard's opinion on anything, he must always reply with that question. If he admits he wasn't paying attention, or if he were to give an answer that was in opposition to what she was saying, that could cause an argument.

Arguments are hard in relationships, but they're dangerous in affairs. What if he pisses her off, and she decides to come clean about what they're doing? What if she's angry, and she makes a little phone call to his wife? What if? What if? What if?

There are so many ways she could screw him, and none of them right now involve the two of them being naked. His office has rules about people 'dipping their pen in the company ink', and Howard could lose his job.

In one act of anger, she could cause him to lose his wife, his unborn child, his home, and his livelihood. Dangerous, eh?

Howard listens as Claire bores him senseless with a story about some pop-star who demanded orphans be on stage with her because puppies were no-longer cute enough. Howard starts to chew the inside of his cheek as a way to help him concentrate. The pain brings about focus.

Silence. This is Howard's signal to respond. Once again Howard has tuned out Claire's voice. Only thing is, this time, unlike all the others, Howard just doesn't give a fuck.

'I don't know' Howard's response is curt and anger filled, even though he didn't raise his voice. A very dangerous thing has occurred, a very volatile situation has developed; Howard has stopped caring.

'What was that, honey?' the violated angel asks. The light is hitting her face just at the right angle, and she is at this moment in time the most beautiful woman who ever lived on this God-for-saken planet.

Howard is looking straight at her face, almost actually staring through it, his mind consumed by thoughts of what Claire might have been doing, or will do, with unknown men. Howard is looking at the person who makes him happier than anyone else ever has, and yet she's making him angrier than he's ever been.

'I said I don't know' Howard is being honest. Far too honest for anyone's good, 'And to be completely honest I don't even care.' There is not even the slightest trace of joviality in his voice.

Claire doesn't know what to think. She's never seen Howard being anything other than a perfect gentleman, not including the times he's thrown her over the tables and gone at her like a hungry lion attacking an unsuspecting zebra on the planes of the Serengeti.

'I, what-' Claire doesn't know what to say, her beloved Howard was speaking to her, if it can be called that, in a tone she wasn't used to from him.

'I don't care!' Howard interrupts her. Why, he figures, should I bother with politeness and manners when this little whore's putting it about all over? No, Howard is not thinking rationally.

'What's wrong with you, Howard?' the angel inquires.

'Me? What's wrong with me? I don't know, what is wrong with me?' Howard's getting angrier and angrier. Right now, it's anybody's guess as to just why he's getting so angry.

Howard could be getting so angry because his beautiful, violated angel has cheated on him. Because he thought that they had something special and she's thrown it all away by doing something with someone who is isn't Howard.

Or it could be that Howard really isn't angry at Claire, this vision of perfection, at all. It could be that he's angry at himself, for allowing himself to become so emotionally attached to, as he used to refer to her, 'just a secretary'.

It could be that Howard's anger is masking pain and sorrow. Not the pain and sorrow of being rejected by someone he cares for deeply, but the pain and sorrow brought about by feelings of inadequacy.

Howard's thinking, 'If in was any good at this, I'd be able to keep her happy and fulfilled' And this, this, is the source of Howard's anger. He feels he's not being able to satisfy Claire, and that's why she's screwing around behind his back.

'Fuck you, you whore-bitch!' Howard has officially lost the plot. Howard storms over to the beautiful angel and grabs her forcefully by the shoulders, momentarily rocking her backwards with the force.

'How could you do this to me?' Howard isn't just asking a question, he's demanding an answer. The veins in his neck and temples have been pushed to the surface and they appear to almost want to break out the skin. His nostrils are flared, his eyes are bulging out of his skull.

Claire is terrified. She is far too confused as to what's happening to even realise how scared she is. She hurts her jaw trying to open her mouth as wide as it can possibly go, in the vain hope that the more distance between her top and bottom lip the more chance there is of her being able to say something.

Howard lifts Claire from the bed, sending her cigarette spiralling to the blood red, satin sheets, splaying the ash like a tiny, miniature firework.

Howard drags Claire across the room to the bathroom, although he doesn't know why. Howard doesn't know just what he's doing, but he damn sure knows why.

Howard gets Claire to the bathroom door, and throws her down to the floor, where she sits, her legs folded under her like they no longer possessed any bones. She is slumped there against the door frame like a weeping child.

Claire is totally confused. 'What's happening? Why is he doing this? What's gotten into him? Why is he behaving like this? What did I do wrong?' All would be perfectly reasonable questions, only Claire's mind's running at a thousand miles per hour, in total contrast to her mouth, which seems to be stuck.

Then it hits Howard, the perfect way to show Claire that he's not the man to screw around on. Howard picks Claire up by grabbing her arms just below the shoulder, leaving unsightly red marks. A perfect print of Howard's hands.

Howard forces Claire backwards through the bathroom, forcing her to trip over her own feet no less than three times. The bathroom is less than seven feet across from wall-to-wall, including the space the bath takes up, and Howard wanders just how the hell she can trip over three times!

Claire has stopped being pushed backwards now, and she can feel the cold bathtub against the back of her naked thighs. Maybe she'd be less worried about what's going on if she could see, but her vision's blurred from the tears, which storm down her beautiful cheeks like salty slug trails.

Howard's left hand clasps Claire's tiny, perfect neck like a vice. Even now, as his head is filled with those thoughts, Howard is distracted by how smooth her perfect skin in. Howard remembers how last night, the blood red satin sheets were coarse in comparison to his perfect, violated angel's skin.

The hotel's emblem swishes through the air as Howard's right hand brings the heavy glass ashtray up to meet Claire's perfectly contoured skull.

The sick THUD! of the ash container meeting flesh and bone, resonates in Howard's ears, as the blood splatters onto his face with a stomach churning squelch. Then, realising just what it is he's actually done, Howard brings the ashtray up through the air again and again, until the beautiful angel's limp body slumps backwards into the bath.

Howard drops the ashtray onto Claire's still body, then suddenly reaches for the shower tap. There are two, gleaming stainless steel taps protruding from the white tiled wall, and yet it's taking Howard close to a minute to find the right tap.

Howard's taking his time, due largely to the fact that he isn't looking at what his hand's doing. Howard's focus of interest is Claire. Or rather, what used to be Claire's body.

The cold water juts outs of the steel shower head before firing a steady, constant stream of increasingly hotter water directly at the angel's body. The blood runs along the white bathtub and swirls down the drain like a cheap, rip off horror film.

And then it happens. All of it, in one foul, wretched swoop. The adrenaline dump first, making Howard's entire body shake with what he is mistaking for fear. Howard is now trying desperately to figure out what it is he's afraid of.

Then the reality of what he's done. He has taken a human life. He has wilfully killed another living person purely because he let his petty jealousy get the better of him. A person has been killed because Howard isn't secure in himself as a lover.

Howard is now trembling, repeating to himself that is didn't really happen. But Howard knows damn well it did. Claire's lifeless body in the tub being pelted with blasting jets of water will remind him of that.

Howard's emotions are beginning to get the better of him. His eyes are glazing over with tears as he's repeating to the perfectly still body the violated angel, twisted and contorted in the iron tub.

It's been a solid fifteen minutes since the ashtray first struck Claire's head, sending a stream of blood up, through and across the angel's golden-blonde hair. And all Howard can think as he recalls the incident in the smallest of details is how the red slashes through Claire's hair were richer and deeper, but not darker, than the blood red satin sheets.

Howard has now calmed down considerably, and is sitting still, his back propped against the doorway to the bathroom. Howard has his head down, his forehead resting in his right palm. Howard is searching through the dark recesses of his mind, trying to find a solution.

Howard would be able to find a solution if only he could make sense of what had happened.

Then it comes to him. Almost as swiftly as the ashtray had come to Claire's perfect head, the idea, the solution, has come to Howard. He rushes over to the bed and searches through the blood red stain sheets. Howard stands back from the bed, and lifts the wrinkled top sheet until he hears a thud.

Howard bends down and picks up the silver lighter, with

James Dean's face etched onto it, up off the floor, and takes it into the bathroom.

Howard turns the water off. Then, for now Howard has a sense of right and wrong, he goes back into the bedroom.

Howard is smiling maniacally at his ingenious idea. There is a disturbing mixture of his saliva and Claire's splattered blood running down his chin, but none of that matters right now because Howard is doing something he considers to be a good idea.

Howard returns to the bathroom with the wrinkled blood red satin sheets and proceeds to wrap the dripping body of his violated angel in the sheet like a cocoon. Now Howard's lying the body down in the bath, looking like some kind of mummified heavenly body.

Howard kisses Claire's still warm but wounded forehead and places the silver James Dean lighter on the angel's sheet-wrapped chest, then walks back into the bedroom.

Howard doesn't see the point in a note at this time. He thinks it's going to be fairly obvious to everyone and anyone what happened, what was happening in the room. Plus he can't think of what exactly a person writes in these situations.

Howard's hands shake as the bottle of bourbon empties into a shot glass.

Howard sits on the edge of the bed and breathes in deeply through his nose. The first scent to hit him is Claire's perfume rising up from her white shirt, which is laying at his feet on the floor.

Howard's eyes roll backwards into his skull for the minute as his eye lids sink slowly and peacefully down. His mind's eye sees Claire's beautiful, unmatchable smile. He sees the cheeky, seductive wink she'd given him at the office when she knew no one was looking.

He can hear her melodic laughter, and he thinks about how she made him feel loved and wanted and needed and worthy when his own wife would do nothing but hurl abuse at him and then apologise by blaming it on the hormones.

Then, as if his mind was working in chronological order, he sees Claire's perfect face, scrunched up into some ugly, tear-drenched mask, as he brought the ashtray to her temple again and again. Howard's eyes explode open as reality doesn't sneak up on him but rather runs him over like a Mack truck doing the wrong side of 80.

Howard tries to turn his head to look to the bathroom door, as though he's expecting to see his violated angel wearing a white robe and drying her just watched golden-blonde hair. But, he knows that's never going to happen, and his neck is stiff.

Howard stares out of the window, as he brings the shot glass up to his lips and drains the glass as his mind wanders to thoughts of his heavily pregnant wife and what his child will look like, whether his child will be a boy or a girl when it's finally born?

Howard takes one last deep breath, then takes one last long sip of whatever's left in the shot glass in his sweaty palm, then stands up straight and tall and walks to the far side of the bedroom. Howard re-fills the shot glass with some of the champagne left over from last night, and takes the glass into the bathroom and put it on the side of the bath. For the ghost of his fallen angel.

Howard walks into the bedroom, and for a moment everything is still. There are no cares, worries or troubles anywhere on the planet for just that single moment. Then, with one last final act of unbelievable courage, Howard races across the bedroom and throws himself at the bedroom window.

Howard glides, in his own mind, gently through the air, if it wasn't for the wind whistling past his ears, he would swear that he was just…hovering in the air.

Of course, in reality, Howard is hurtling towards the ground below at a violent rate. But, as Howard has already worked out in his mind, this is for the best and the only real option.

The torment, the suffering and the mental anguish that the

few people milling around outside the hotel will endure for the next few weeks is unmentionable. They have just seen a man plummet to his death in front of their very eyes.

And inside the hotel, on the second floor, a heavily pregnant Asian woman is meeting with a man to put a hold on their affair until after the baby's born...

The End.